# Second Wind

# Second Wind

*Ray Hobbs*

Spiderwize

## Second Wind
All Rights Reserved. Copyright © 2011 Ray Hobbs

No part of this book may be reproduced or transmitted in any form or by any means, graphic, electronic, or mechanical, including photocopying, recording, taping or by any information storage or retrieval system, without the permission in writing from the copyright holder.

The right of Ray Hobbs to be identified as the author of this work has been asserted in accordance with the Copyright, Designs and Patents Act 1988 sections 77 and 78.

Spiderwize
Office 404, 4th Floor
Albany House
324/326 Regent Street
London
W1B 3HH
UK

www.spiderwize.com

This is a work of fiction. Names, characters and incidents are products of the author's imagination. Any resemblance to persons living or dead is entirely coincidental.

The views expressed in this work are solely those of the author and do not necessarily reflect the views of the publisher, and the publisher hereby disclaims any responsibility for them.

ISBN: 978-1-908128-30-0

This book is dedicated to the memory of the late Malcolm Laycock, whose BBC Radio Two programme delighted listeners for fourteen years with the sounds of the British dance bands. He is greatly missed.

# Acknowledgements

Writing is a solitary occupation, and I should never have completed this book without the patience, understanding and support of my wife Sheila, who saw very little of me at times, but who was always ready with suggestions, particularly from the female perspective.

Occupied though I was, I still appreciated the silent companionship of Millie, who was with me almost to the final revision, and of Phoebe and Amy, who still visit me occasionally to assure me that I am not forgotten, and to remind me that writers, as well as dogs, need exercise.

I am also indebted to my brother Chris, who acted as sounding board from planning stage to completion, who was a ready and reliable source of suggestions and encouragement and who, most importantly, never stopped believing.

# Glossary for Readers Outside the UK

| | |
|---|---|
| Guildhall | Guildhall School of Music & Drama, London |
| Nipper | Young child |
| Bar (in music) | Measure |
| Bum | Posterior |
| Pint | An imperial pint (20 fluid ounces), in this case, of beer, usually referred to as 'bitter' or 'mild' |
| Bloke | Guy |
| Crotchet | Quarter note |
| Quaver | Eighth note |
| Rubber | Eraser |
| Mill | Factory making woollen cloth |
| Biscuit | Cookie |
| WAAF | Women's Auxiliary Air Force (World War Two) |
| Received Pronunciation | Absurdly correct English diction once adopted by actors and broadcasters |
| Tea Dance | Afternoon entertainment with tea, sandwiches and cakes, popular before WW2 |
| O.A.P. | Old-age pensioner, now known as a senior citizen |
| Handbag | Purse |
| (Royal) British Legion | Voluntary care organisation for ex-service personnel |
| Mate | Pal, buddy |
| RSPCA | Royal Society for the Prevention of Cruelty to Animals |
| Solicitor | Attorney |

| | |
|---|---|
| Beak | Magistrate, a minor justice |
| Dripping | Rendered-down beef fat. Long ago, people on low incomes spread it on bread. Just as horrible as it sounds |
| A.T.S. | Auxiliary Territorial Service. Women's army in WW2 |
| Land girl | Member of the Women's Land Army, who worked on farms in WW2, freeing men for military service |
| Spiv | Small-time black market dealer in WW2, often dressed extravagantly |
| (Sir) Alf Ramsey | Manager of the England football team that won the World Cup in 1966 |
| Bobby | Police officer. Nicknamed after Sir Robert Peel, founder of the British police force. |

# 1
# A West Yorkshire Town
# 1990

Frank Morrison felt like a truant with the unusual luxury of a good excuse. He should have been working on the music score of *Honey for Tea*, but he was much happier taking Kate to the orchestra practice at the Wool Exchange.

He'd spent the past hour searching for two strong, contrasting themes that would work eventually in counterpoint and, as concentration seemed to have deserted him, he was relieved when Kate said that she wanted to look up some of her old friends in the orchestra. It also pleased Frank that, at nineteen and with all the distractions of student life, she still wanted to do that, and in their shared optimism they were particularly unprepared for the scene they discovered when they entered the Wool Exchange ballroom.

Where they had expected to see around thirty-five musicians, only a dozen or so occupied the seats set out for the orchestra. Some talked quietly together; a few simply gazed at the floor or at nothing in particular, their instrument cases beside them, still unopened. Most eloquent of all, though, were the empty chairs behind them.

'Hutch' Hutchins saw them and beckoned them over.

'I'm glad to see you two,' he said. 'You've brought the average age of this gathering down to a mere seventy. Not that it helps us much now, but at least we don't feel completely ostracised by the young and ambitious.' A wisp of white hair had fallen from its parting and it hung over his forehead as if in a forlorn effort to mask its owner's hurt.

Frank surveyed the empty chairs sombrely. Even in the circumstances, his appearance was deceptively severe, and an outsider might have considered him out of place in the faded art deco ballroom, with his dark, drooping moustache and shoulder-length hair. 'So they've finally done it,' he said.

'They've done it all right.' Geoff Brierley was controlling his anger with difficulty. 'But no one bothered to tell us. They just didn't turn up. They'll be having their own practice somewhere else, you can bet.'

There were sounds of agreement from the others, who were only suppressing their anger, Frank imagined, because of Kate, who stood tight-lipped beside him.

'Anyway, Katie,' said Hutch, making an effort for courtesy's sake, 'it's good to see you again. How's it going at the Guildhall?'

Kate looked in disbelief around the familiar, old-fashioned ballroom, with its scallop-fronted bandstand and draped curtains, thoughts of music school clearly far from her mind.

'I never thought they'd go through with this,' she said. 'I thought all that stuff about a breakaway orchestra was just empty talk.'

Hutch nodded. 'We thought so too. They must have been planning it all the time. No wonder there's been so little interest in the anniversary.'

'The anniversary?'

'The orchestra's seventieth birthday next month,' said Frank.

'That's right.' In spite of everything there was still a trace of pride in Hutch's voice. 'It met for the first time in nineteen-twenty, on the tenth of May, and it gave its first concert two weeks later, on Empire Day. I don't remember it myself because I was only a nipper at the time, but one or two of these lads might.'

'Seventy years,' said Geoff, 'and that lot have just swept it aside as if it meant nothing at all.' His anger had turned for the moment to bitterness and he joined the others in glaring at the floor, as if the boards themselves were to blame.

'I was there,' the man beside Geoff said to no one in particular. 'I must have been eight when my mother brought me. They played selections from *The Pirates of Penzance* and *The Merry Widow*. It's funny, you know, there are times when I've all on to remember what happened yesterday, but I recall that programme as clearly as anything.' He looked up and caught Kate's eye. 'The musicians were nearly all women,' he told her. 'Men were in short supply after the first war, you see, and the women used to take it in turns to look after the kiddies while the others rehearsed.' He smiled faintly at the memory. 'You had to take your hat off to those lasses, organising themselves like that, with all they had to do at work and at home. They used to give monthly concerts here in this ballroom, and the Exchange Club let them have it free of charge because the proceeds went to the war widows and disabled of the town.'

'That wasn't all they did,' said Geoff. 'I wonder how many musicians got their first orchestral experience here. Most of us here did, and then there's Frank and Katie.' He nodded in their direction. 'That's three generations.' He held up three fingers and then lowered his hand in disgust. 'And now our generation's on the scrap heap.'

Geoff's companion stood up and lifted his double bass upright in its case. 'I'll see you lads around,' he said quietly.

'Take it easy, Kenneth,' said Hutch.

When he was out of the room one of them said, 'Poor old Kenneth. He goes back further than any of us.'

As they lapsed into what seemed to be a general reflection on that observation, Frank looked at Kate and her expression told him that it was time to leave.

She was uncharacteristically quiet through lunch at her favourite restaurant, and it wasn't until they were back at the flat that she became more communicative.

'What are you working on now, Dad?'

'*Honey for Tea*. It's a two-part drama.'

'Another one about the First World War?'

He shook his head. 'This one's set just after the war. It's about unemployment, disillusionment and that sort of thing.'

'It doesn't sound very cheerful.'

'It doesn't, does it? Still, the main character has his moments, and it ends cheerfully enough.'

'Good.' She ran her forefinger absently around the rim of her coffee mug. 'I'm glad something has a happy ending.' It was clear that the orchestra was still on her mind, because after a moment she asked, 'Did the other lot ever ask you to join them?'

'Yes, ages ago when the idea first came up.'

'I hope you told them to stuff it.' Irritably, she swept a lock of fair hair from her eyes. 'I just don't understand why they had to do it. It was completely out of order.'

He gave her hand a squeeze. 'I know,' he said. 'I've known those blokes nearly thirty years and I feel the same as you, but we can't ignore the fact that when musicians grow old they lose their edge. For one thing, they don't react as quickly as they used to.'

'I know,' she said. 'You're thinking about *The Yeomen of the Guard,* aren't you? If you remember, I was in the orchestra for that.'

He nodded. 'So you'll remember the soprano who kept coming in two bars early.'

'Oh, yes.'

'And the conductor signalled the band to skip two bars.'

'That's right. All but two did and it sounded like nothing on earth.' She put her mug down impatiently. 'But they don't expect to be asked to play for the shows at their age.' Her eyes were suddenly wet. 'It's so cruel and unfair. They lived for the practices and the concerts. It's their way of life, the only way they know, and now that's all been taken from them.' She was silent for a moment and then she pulled a ball of crumpled tissues from the pocket of her jeans to dab her eyes. 'I can't forget the way those poor old men looked this morning. It was horrible.'

'They're tougher than you think, Kate. Most of them have been through much worse than this. They'll carry on somehow.'

'But it won't be the same. Nothing ever stays the same.' Her voice began to waver. 'Dad, isn't there something you can do?'

...

He was working on the score two weeks later, when he came to the end of Part One, where the central character, now recovered from his exhaustion, had found the strength for a fling with the farmer's wife who had taken him in. The world of make-believe was truly wonderful, especially as a respite from the horrors that real life threw at people. It was little wonder it was so popular. Even Kate, usually so self possessed, had recently turned to the magical last resort of her childhood.

*Dad, isn't there something you can do?*

He left his desk and moved nearer the window so that he could see beyond the reflection of the room. Apart from the hiss of an occasional car on the wet road and the sound of running footsteps, everything was quiet outside. Presently, the owner of the footsteps materialised in a dark tracksuit and Frank felt a twinge of disappointment. He was used to seeing her in daylight, when she usually wore shorts and a white top, an ensemble he found much more appealing.

As she reached the end of Providence Road and vanished from Frank's view, his gaze fell on the joinery and carpet warehouse there that had once been the public baths. At least the sand-blasted shell of the Victorian building had been allowed to remain. Others had been demolished to make room for car parks and mini trading estates. Even the old market place was now a piazza linking Alfred Street and Cheapside. The signs of progress were everywhere: the new ousting the old. Like the new, leaner, fitter orchestra.

He pondered that for a while, half conscious of the work waiting to be done. He still had time to work on the score though, and he owed it to Kate, Hutch and the others to think of something that might at least ease the hurt.

Looking up at his portrait gallery on the studio wall, he noticed that Wyatt Earp looked far from encouraging; General Custer seemed disinterested, his mind most likely on more important matters, and it was anyone's guess what Billy the Kid was thinking. It was a bloody awful picture, and Frank had only hung him there because he felt sorry for him.

He looked again at the list of names he had made, and then at the instruments they represented. At first sight there was the usual embarrassment of clarinets but he knew that three of them could double on alto or tenor saxophone. He re-drew the list, grouping the same instruments together so that it made sense of the one idea he'd had so far. It read:

*2 clarinets*
*3 saxes (2 with Hutch in front)*
*2 trumpets (including me)*
*1 trombone, (2 with Norman back)*
*1 violin (2 with Kate at home)*
*1 percussionist*
*1 guitar (possibly, but Fred might be more useful on piano for now)*
*1 bass (possibly)*

It was the photograph of Penny and Tim taken twenty years earlier in the Blackpool Tower Ballroom that had set the thought in motion. He looked again at his sister, pretty and graceful in the sapphire-blue dress their mother had made for her, and at Tim, self-conscious in the ex-hire dress suit that he'd bought for the televised championships. Dancing was popular with spectators as well as participants in those days, and whilst Frank had no idea what had happened to the spectators he knew that people still danced. He'd seen posters in Kate's old school, advertising evening classes in Ballroom and Latin, and he understood that there was never any lack of interest. It was just a shame that the participants never had the opportunity to dance to live music.

But there were band parts buried in the orchestra library that hadn't been used for years. He'd seen some of them within the past few months when he was looking for music for a concert. He remembered the musty scent of old paper and the thumbed and dog-eared pages. One of the parts was scorched along the top, no doubt the result of an encounter with a desk lamp. Most vividly of all though, he recalled the purple, rubber-stamped names of their original owners. Some were strange and exotic: The Novelty Kinema, The New Electric Theatre and The Picture Palace. Others were of bands that had played in hotels, restaurants and dance halls, and as he thought of them the sounds of the instruments came to his composer's ear: the warm tones of saxophones overlaid with clarinets, muted brass and strings. They were the romantic sounds of the great pre-war bands, sounds that deserved to be heard again, and best of all, they called for something approximating to the line-up left behind by the breakaway orchestra.

That was assuming that the old boys were ready to play again. Only a couple of weeks had passed since that wretched morning, and recent communications with the new orchestra had only opened the wound further.

On the other hand, though, some of the lads had been brought up on dance music, so it wasn't as if they'd be breaking completely new ground. After a little more thought he pulled his address book out of the desk drawer to look up Hutch's number.

# 2

Four centuries of prominent clothiers frowned down from their gilt frames as Frank and Kate climbed the wide staircase to the Wool Exchange ballroom, as if they were still unable to accept that the Exchange Club had conferred honorary membership on a company of musicians. It had been a special relationship as well, for the Club to have welcomed the orchestra there from its earliest days.

When Frank and Kate entered the ballroom they found several of their number already there, but the atmosphere was subdued and there was little evidence of willingness to start.

'Hello, Frank,' Hutch shook his hand. 'Hello, Katie. It's good to see you both.'

'Hi, Hutch.' Kate extended her hand and dodged sideways to avoid having her hair ruffled. Being called 'Katie' was bad enough.

'Well, here they are.' He gestured towards the group of musicians. 'Two of the lads have brought their alto saxes, just as you asked, but I don't know how it's going to go. It's maybe a bit soon to be trying this.'

'Let's find out anyway.'

'They're still feeling very low, Frank. Are you going to stand in front, by the way?'

'No, that's your job.' Frank lifted his trumpet case. 'I've come to play.'

'Good. You can play the solos.' He turned and called, 'Right lads, let's get set up.'

More out of habit than motivation, the musicians set out the chairs and music stands, took out their instruments and tuned. Frank looked around him apprehensively. There was a fair chance that Hutch was right about it being too soon for something new.

Hutch stood before them, arms folded. 'We've been through a rotten time,' he said, 'but it's something we've got to put behind us.' He gestured towards the music on their stands. 'To help us do that, and while the rest of us have been looking for a rope to hang ourselves, young Frank's been giving some thought to what we can do with the line-up we've got, and as it's the first positive idea I've heard I think we ought to give it a try. Most of us have played this stuff at some time so we're not learning new tricks.' He glanced around at the orchestra. 'Right,' he said, '"Honeysuckle Rose". To get us into the mood I'll count you in.'

Several eyebrows rose, so he said patiently, 'I know you don't need it, but let's try, at the very least, to have a bit of fun. A-one, two, three, four...'

Frank picked up his trumpet and listened to the four bars of introduction. He knew then that it would be heavy going. There was nothing technically wrong with their playing but it was evident that enthusiasm was sleeping late that Sunday morning.

'Stop.' Hutch put his stick down and stared at them. 'You can do better than that. It's a romantic number, not a funeral march.'

Some of them exchanged glances and they tried again but with little improvement.

'Sorry, Hutch.' Geoff Brierley rested his trombone to speak. 'You know how we're all feeling. You can't expect us to bounce back just like that.'

'Geoff's right,' said Vernon Waterhouse. 'You've been to a lot of trouble, Frank. It were a nice thought, lad, and don't think it isn't appreciated, but I don't think any of us is in the mood for starting afresh.'

Frank bit his lip at the murmur of agreement from the others and he was about to put his trumpet away when Hutch spoke again.

'I'm not expecting anybody to bounce back,' he said, 'and the last thing I expected was wild enthusiasm. I just wanted you to give the idea a fair try after all the work Frank's put in on these arrangements. I imagine he had other things to do with his time but he did all this for our benefit, and I think we should show some of that appreciation Vernon was talking about, by making a bit of an effort.' His voice had risen towards the end of the last sentence but now he seemed more disappointed than angry. 'And there's one more thing to bear in mind,' he said. 'We're all supposed to be professionals, and that means that we don't need to be in "the mood", or any kind of mood, for that matter, to do justice to the music.' He nodded towards the door. 'Anyone who's still of a mind can shove off now if he wants to but I'm staying here and you're equally welcome to stay with me. It's up to you.' He folded his arms and waited, and Frank also waited, for his part in painful embarrassment as the others examined their fingernails and blew invisible dust from their instruments.

Eventually Vernon said, 'All right then, let's give it another try.'

There was a cautious murmur of assent and Hutch picked up his stick. 'Now,' he said, 'once more from the top, and this time *with feeling.*'

They played with some improvement and managed to maintain it for the remainder of the practice but Frank wasn't optimistic. He shared his thoughts with Kate as they left the building.

'I can't see them coming back next week,' he said. 'They'd made up their minds before ever they started.

'I was just thinking what a shame it was that Norman Barraclough wasn't here. He'd have stirred things up.'

'He probably would, but if they can't find their own enthusiasm the idea doesn't stand a chance.' He stopped to unlock the car. 'They're like a team that's been stuffed once too often. They've just stopped believing in themselves.'

He started the car and looked at his watch. He had to get Kate home for lunch with her grandparents, and after the morning's events he was particularly thankful that he was no longer expected to join them. Lunch with the in-laws would have been too much to endure.

It had always seemed to him that Helen's parents had a remarkable capacity for making little things seem important, and it was usually the negative things, as they saw them, that mattered most. They ranged from sex on television to daisies on the lawn, and included the length of Frank's hair, his untidy moustache, his disinclination to find a proper job, his fecklessness in encouraging Kate to follow his example, and worst of all, his acquisition of expensive non-essentials, such as a coffee grinder, a dishwasher and a separate phone for his studio. One telephone, they told him, was quite sufficient for most people.

After twenty years, the list seemed endless and he'd long since given up trying to appease them, but now it no longer mattered. His marriage to Helen was effectively over, and however he felt about that, at least his life would be free from their critical scrutiny.

...

Geoff put two pints on the table and sat down. 'I feel bad,' he said, 'thinking about young Frank doing all that for us, and then all that was said.' It was quite early, and the cosy Victorian lounge bar of *The Coach and Horses* was empty but for the two of them.

'What *we* said,' Vernon corrected him, 'both of us.'

'I'm not denying it. I'm saying I feel bad.'

'It wasn't bad when we finally got going,' said Vernon, 'although I must say we could have played better. I wish we had now, if only for Frank's sake.'

'Aye.' Geoff looked thoughtful. 'You used to play with a dance band, didn't you, Vernon?'

'I played with a few. They were good times; all too brief, but good while they lasted.' He lifted his glass at the memory. 'I did a bit of all sorts after the war but I never got the same satisfaction. The style of dance music in the fifties wasn't really to my taste. Of course, we still played the old songs as well, but that was when singers started buggering about with them instead of singing them as they were meant to be sung. They do it all the time now.'

'I'll say they do,' said Geoff, 'and you're right about the quality. There was a feeling, an atmosphere that you just don't get nowadays.'

Vernon nodded wistfully. 'It were grand. You had clarinets and saxes in unison, brass and reed choruses in block harmony, and singers who sang as if they meant it. They were the things that made a romantic number.'

Geoff's career had been a progression from the pit of one theatre to the next; his experience of the ballroom had been restricted to the dance floor, but something in the lacklustre efforts of that morning had triggered a few memories for him too. After a little more thought, he said, 'I don't suppose there's any reason why we shouldn't give it another try, Vernon. What do you think?'

...

Hutch held the phone to his ear for maybe ten seconds, wondering if there might be a fault on the line, and then Norman Barraclough spoke again and it was obvious that he had been giving Hutch's news some thought.

'I'll tell you what, Hutch,' he said, 'I'm sorry I wasn't there.'

'It's all right,' Hutch told him. 'We knew you had commitments.'

'I'm not apologising. I mean I wish I'd been there, because I'd have had a thing or two to say. What numbers did you play?'

Hutch gathered his thoughts. 'Let's see. There was "Night and Day", "Anything Goes", "You Do Something to Me", and let me think—'

'Do you mean to tell me they were still dragging their feet after playing that lot?'

'They didn't find it easy,' Hutch admitted, also wishing now that Norman had been at the practice.

'Hey, but trust young Frank to come up with something like this. I reckon we can form a fair old dance band, and it's back to where we started out, Hutch, thee and me – you on tenor sax and little Vernon on clarinet and alto sax.'

'I was conducting,' Hutch reminded him.

'We'll get you back on tenor sax, don't you worry. Let's get another practice set up before we've all forgotten how to enjoy ourselves.'

. . .

It was ten past seven on Monday evening and Frank decided to stop work. He was pleased with his progress but his eyes were tired and he was finding it hard to focus on the score. He rubbed his eyes and turned his head this way and that to ease the stiffness in his neck before fetching a can of beer from the kitchen.

The smell of roast beef had been tantalising on Sunday lunchtime when he'd sat in the kitchen talking with Helen, and he was pleased that he was no longer affected by the sight of her bum wiggling when she mixed the gravy. It was an indication of the progress he'd made since the separation. Of course, that wasn't to say that he no longer found her attractive. She still had a lovely, trim figure and shapely legs too; and now he thought of it, he was thankful that Kate had inherited Helen's physical characteristics rather than his. She might have had his cleft chin or, worse still, the poor kid might have been eight inches taller and built like a brick weaving shed. OK, she'd have been fearsome in a netball scrum, or whatever they called it, and she'd have had no difficulty getting served in a crowded bar, but there were other things in life, so he was glad Helen's genes had won that skirmish.

He looked up at Wyatt Earp and the great lawman appeared to agree. He also seemed to suggest to Frank that he should finish his beer and get himself another, and Frank had just done that when the phone rang.

'Frank, it's Pat-sy.' Patsy Daniels of Orion TV Productions always inflected her greeting as if she were singing it. It came out as a dotted crotchet and three quavers. Frank didn't have perfect pitch but he imagined the notes to be E-E-A-G. One day when he had nothing better to do he might check them on the piano.

'Lovely to hear from you, Patsy. What's the matter, can't you sleep?'

'Oh, come on, it's not that late.'

'If you say so. How can I help?'

'How's the score going?'

'Pretty well. I've sketched most of the titles. There's a bit of fine tuning to do and then the donkey work begins.'

'What's that?'

'The orchestration.'

'How big is the orchestra?' The question had an edge to it.

'Thirty, as we agreed, but it's still a lot of work, even with a small orchestra.'

'Ah well, that's a complete mystery to me but I'll look forward to hearing it all the same.' After a second's pause she said, 'Frank, there's another job coming up if you're interested.'

'I'm always interested.'

'That's what I thought. It's for Anvil Productions, a fairly new outfit based in the Midlands. A protégé of mine set it up and I help them with the odd thing from time to time. I said I'd speak to you.'

'What's it about?'

'It's a two-part series based on the idea of *Three Men in a Boat* but it's set in the fifties. There's some romantic interest in it as well.'

'It sounds interesting. I'm game if they want me.'

'Good. I'll tell them.'

'Thanks, Patsy.'

'My pleasure. I'll be in touch. Bye-ee.' She sang the last word on a falling minor third, like the first two notes of the 'Colonel Bogey' theme, and some people might have found that jarring, but Frank was fond of Patsy. Also, she'd found him another production, and he was sick to death of making his living from commercials and arrangements of bloody awful pop ballads. It was one good thing at a time when it was sorely needed. In a perfect world it would be followed by two more but he was content for the time being. He raised his can of beer to share the moment with Wyatt Earp and the others, and the phone rang again.

It was Hutch, and he sounded unexpectedly cheerful.

# 3

When Frank arrived at the Exchange the following Sunday he found Hutch in the library blowing the dust from a set of band parts.

'What are you looking for, Hutch?'

'Fast and lively numbers for now, Frank, just to build up a bit of confidence. The lads are coming round, as I told you, but we need to tread carefully.' He took out another folder and put it with his collection. 'The older stuff seems to appeal to most of them.'

'Older than what?'

'Pre-war, basically.'

Frank ran his finger over the shelf marked *Slow Foxtrots*. 'I suppose we can forget these for now.'

'I'd rather leave them for later.' Hutch went on with his search and then looked up again. 'Wait a minute though, can you find "Memories of You" over there?'

'Let's see.' Frank riffled through the dust-covered folders. 'Yes, here it is.' He handed Hutch the set, and the older man nodded.

'This'll make a good start if we don't take it too slow. Norman'll tell you that. It's one of his favourites.' He looked again at what he'd collected so far and said, 'I think we've enough to be going on with. Let's get things started.

Even seated, Norman Barraclough towered over the rest of the band. He was a big man with a bass voice that matched his frame.

'"Memories of You"? I hope we're not going to play it like Benny Goodman used to or we'll all be asleep before the second chorus.'

'All right,' said Hutch, 'give us your tempo.'

'Beat a lively two in a bar, Hutch. One, two, one two,' he demonstrated. 'It worked for Bill Cotton.'

'Hang on a minute,' Martin Hirst interrupted, 'have I got this solo at bar thirty or not? Somebody's scribbled through it.'

'Bar thirty.' Hutch found it in the score. 'Yes, first violin solo. We've no singer so it has to be. Do you want to rub it out?' He felt in his pocket for a rubber.

'No thanks, I can busk this.'

Hutch counted them in and the number began. On the front row, Frank was beginning to enjoy himself. The playing was much more confident than before, and he sensed the same pleasure around him, especially when Martin went into his solo. He played with a full, rich tone, syncopating the melody against the strict beat of the rhythm section. Then the clarinets and saxophones swung into their chorus, soothing and beguiling, until the brass section joined them in a strutting phrase that rang out with new ebullience.

At the end, Norman rested his trombone and said, 'Not bad for a start. Our section needs to work on that last chorus to get it really tight, and we need a bass an' all.'

'I know,' said Hutch. 'Kenneth won't come back. The business with the new orchestra's finished him for good.'

'It was only to be expected, but what happened to Maurice? We haven't seen him for a while.'

'Last I heard he was having a rupture operation. He should be over it now though. It was a couple of months ago.'

'Do you think he'd come back?'

'There's only one way to find out. I'll give him a ring later.'

'It were that concert of film music last autumn that did it,' said Geoff. 'The bass part in the "Spitfire Fugue" gets a bit hectic in places, and I reckon that's when he caught his wedding tackle with the end of his bow...' He stopped and looked around anxiously. 'Little Katie isn't here, is she?'

'Relax,' said Frank. 'She's back in London.' It was a shame she wasn't there to experience the new mood. He had it in mind to tell her about it as soon as possible.

'While we're on the subject of deficiencies,' Fred Adams called from the piano, 'do you think we could get a regular pianist? I don't mind helping out occasionally but you called me in because you wanted a guitarist.'

'All right, all right.' Hutch held up his hands in appeal. 'If you like, we'll have a meeting after the practice, but let's get on for heaven's sake. I want us to play "Memories of You" again, and then we've a few more numbers to try.'

After the practice, Norman eased himself into one of the buttoned leather armchairs in the Club lounge. 'They're coming on better than I expected,' he said. 'It was a good idea of yours, Frank. If you hadn't come up with it we'd still have been scratching our arses and feeling miserable, and that doesn't do anybody any good, does it, flower?' He addressed the last three words to the small dog that had settled between his feet with her chin resting on one burnished toe-cap. She swivelled her eyes upward at the sound of his voice, then settled once more until Norman looked up again and saw Hutch and Geoff arriving. 'About time too,' he remarked. 'We were dying of thirst.'

Hutch put down the drinks he was carrying and produced a packet of pork scratchings.

'Murderous on the fillings, them things,' Norman told him.

'I'm not wasting these on the likes of you. They're for Ida.' He pulled the packet open and gave a piece to the dog, who took it daintily at first and then devoured it under the table. Frank watched her hoover up the crumbs and station herself expectantly by Hutch's knee. Her parentage was obscure; he sometimes thought he recognised some West Highland features, but knowing as little as he did about dogs he couldn't be sure.

'What's on your mind, Frank?' asked Hutch. 'You're having one of your quiet spells.'

'Oh, nothing much. I was just thinking that we ought to sort out some more numbers so that I can arrange them for our line-up.' He looked at them uncertainly and added, 'That's if that you want me to do the arranging?'

'We can't think of anyone we'd rather have do it,' said Hutch.

'And we'll find some numbers for you to arrange,' said Norman, 'now that we're starting – just starting, mind – to sound like a band.'

'Good.' Frank caught sight of Ida again under the table. 'Can she have a drink, Norman?'

'She'll sulk all day if she doesn't get one.'

Frank took the clean ashtray from the table and carefully decanted some of his beer into it. 'There, Ida.' He set it down for her and smiled as she lapped industriously.

...

A few days later, he took a short cut through the Memorial Park to the post office. It always seemed to him that the park was delightfully out of place in Cullington, as if the freshness and colour belonged to a brighter place altogether, such as a seaside resort. He'd held that opinion ever since his first visit to the coast, a day trip to Scarborough when he was ten. Since then he had come to regard the park as a familiar calendar, and because each season had some facet that pleased him he found himself drawn to the place all the year round.

The blooms of early spring were gone now, and the bedding plants were out, brash and vibrant. Before long, there would be more colours to taunt the tired evergreens. It was a fascinating cycle.

The memorial had always appealed to his imagination too. The lone soldier held a rifle in one hand, and the other might have been clenched symbolically in a fist, but viewed from a certain angle it seemed to be engaged with his fly. Frank wondered sometimes if the man had been shot at a moment of personal urgency, because if that were the case it was little wonder he was still clutching himself.

As he studied the memorial again he heard a familiar, deep voice.

'Chin up, Frank, it might never happen.'

He looked up suddenly. 'Hello, Norman. Hello, Ida.' Crouching down, he stroked her behind the ears.

'Where are you bound, Frank?'

'The post office.'

'We might as well walk together.' They fell in step and Norman asked, 'Have you heard from Hutch?'

'Yes, he phoned me yesterday and told me about Eddie.'

'That's right. Eddie's going to give the band a try. He's not promising anything in the long-term but it means we've got a pianist for the time being.'

'It might be good for him. How long is it since Dorothy died?'

'It must be nearly six months now. I'm inclined to agree, and it'll get Fred back on guitar.'

'Hutch's been busy.'

'That's not all.' Norman stopped to let Ida pee on the nearest patch of grass. 'Maurice is over his operation and he's coming back, so we'll have a bass again.'

'Excellent.'

'You can say that again. Aye, there's nothing like the old stuff. You know, Frank, it did more for a troubled generation than anything today's youngsters can buy on the streets, and it was a damned sight healthier.' He gave Ida's lead a gentle tug. 'Leave it, Ida.' With her once more at his heel he went on. 'You'd be surprised how many families had been left fatherless after the first war, not that I need to tell you what that's like—'

'Never mind, go on.'

'Right.' Norman mustered his thoughts again. 'That was one problem, and of course there was the unemployment.' He paused for a moment to reflect. 'You see, I've always taken the line that problems are there to be faced, and as a general rule that's true, but you know, sometimes, when there's nothing you can do, you need a distraction, and that's where music and dancing came in. The upper crust, those who could still afford it, danced at the clubs and restaurants, and we lesser mortals gathered at someone's house where they had a wireless set or maybe even a gramophone, and you know, as far as we were concerned we might have been at the Savoy or the Piccadilly. It was a time to forget our troubles, at least 'til the next day, Frank, and it worked. You just couldn't beat it.'

It sounded to Frank like the greatest luxury of all.

'Some suffered worse than others,' said Norman, 'but we all felt it to some extent. I remember the mill going on to two days a week. It was the week after my twenty-first birthday and I couldn't see things improving in a right big hurry. That's when I picked up my trombone and went looking for work, and it wasn't long before Hutch followed me, but that's another story.' He broke off to remonstrate with Ida. 'Will you come out of there?' He twitched her lead again, bringing her to heel. 'I don't know what she finds so fascinating under these bushes.'

Frank walked on, hardly aware of what Norman was saying. The next practice would be on Sunday, but not before the union branch meeting. Members of the new orchestra would be there and it wasn't going to be pleasant, but at least the old boys were beginning to recover from the initial shock. They were no longer as fragile.

'I don't think you've heard a word I've been saying,' said Norman, the least fragile of them all. 'You're miles away.'

'Sorry, what did you say?'

'I said we've got to get organised and work up a proper programme instead of pulling out odd numbers here and there. We've got to be professional about it.' Norman had stopped again and Ida was sniffing at the grass beneath a fir tree. 'If we tackle the job properly we're going to put a few noses out of joint, and I'm going to enjoy that.'

# 4

Hutch looked around at the members who had arrived. 'It's like two branches,' he remarked to Frank. 'Look at 'em. One lot on the right, the other on the left, like flaming politicians.'

It was true. The new orchestra was gathered at one end of the ballroom, some of its members appearing unconcerned whilst a few seemed uneasy, perhaps anxious to get through the meeting as quickly and painlessly as possible. At the other end stood the old guard, showing maybe a hint of resentment but, Frank was heartened to see, none of the previous air of defeat.

A few stood chatting in the middle but they eventually drifted back to their respective camps and the polarisation was complete. Hutch called the meeting to order.

'Let's get through the agenda as quickly as we can decently do it, without anger or unpleasantness, please. The band here wants to have a practice this morning, and I've no doubt the new orchestra also has things to do. We'll start with Apologies for Absence.'

He proceeded to work his way through the agenda. There was no disagreement on either side, and it seemed that Frank's fears were not to be realised. That was until Hutch called for Any Other Business.

One young woman, a violinist in the new orchestra raised her hand immediately. 'I'd like us to call a halt to the unpleasantness that's been going on,' she said. 'We're all in the same branch, and I think that some of the things that have been said were ridiculous and childish. Other orchestras have been through the same experience in the past and they've done it without all this animosity.'

'Happen they have,' said Geoff, 'and happen some of their members weren't subjected to snide remarks and being lampooned in the pit of the Playhouse.' There was a rumble of agreement around him.

'And what about the things you lot have said about us?' demanded a member of the new orchestra. 'I seem to remember phrases like "wet behind the ears" and "jumped-up amateurs".'

'Well, if the cap fits—'

'Ladies and gentlemen, please.' Hutch tapped with his pen on the table. 'This is just what I wanted to avoid. Now listen, everybody. What's done is done, and there's nothing to be gained by going over old ground time and again.'

Geoff was unconvinced. 'If we can't air our grievances here,' he demanded, 'where can we do it?'

'I've told you before, Geoff, the orchestra has nothing to do with the union.'

'Just a minute, Hutch,' Michael Tattersall, conductor of the new orchestra, interrupted him. A courteous and immaculate man even in casual dress, he was a bank manager by full-time occupation, and a natural diplomat. 'We've got to clear the air,' he said. 'It was deplorable that those things happened, and some people have every right to object. I sympathise entirely with anyone who feels slighted, but I also agree with Rosemary that the sooner we get on with what we're supposed to be doing the better it will be for all of us.'

The man beside him nodded vigorously. 'I second that.'

'Good,' said Hutch, 'I'm glad we've got some kind of consensus. Now, has anyone any other business that doesn't involve recrimination, justification, fist-shaking or general buggering about?'

No-one had, but the rift was still there.

With everything set up Hutch addressed the band. 'Now we've got the branch meeting out of the way, thankfully without too much silliness, I'd like to welcome back Maurice and Eddie. It's good to have you with us again.' Everyone greeted the bass player and the pianist, and Hutch was about to begin the practice when he noticed Geoff with his hand up.

'What is it, Geoff?'

'I don't like to keep harping on about it.'

Hutch groaned.

'It's just that we keep talking about the "new orchestra" and it's as if we're encouraging them by giving them a name, if you see what I mean.'

'I don't mind what you call them, Geoff, as long as it's not at a union meeting.'

'Well, I think we ought to be thinking about a special name for ourselves, something with "New" in it as we're doing something different. Don't you think so?'

'I really don't mind,' sighed Hutch. 'Maybe someone would like to think of a name; anything as long as we can get started with this practice. Right,' he said, opening his folder, 'just for a warm-up, let's play "Limehouse Blues".' Vernon Waterhouse looked up in alarm, but Hutch was already counting them in.

They began to play and it was clear straight away that Fred Adams was happy. He was a gregarious man and he had felt isolated behind the Bechstein grand, but he was alone no longer. By contrast, Eddie Young had the appearance of a man of habitual solitude, playing the piano part with deep, frowning concentration. One musician who was not settled, however, was Vernon, and the reason was apparent when he came to the clarinet solo. His old colleagues had been waiting for the kind of brilliant improvisation that had been his former trademark, but instead they heard a fluffed attempt at the solo before he lowered his clarinet.

Hutch cut them off. 'What's up, Vernon?'

Vernon leaned sideways to speak to him. Frank was blocking his line of vision, and at five feet four Vernon was at some disadvantage. 'Sorry Hutch, it's these new National Health dentures.' He pointed unnecessarily to his upper set. 'They're hopeless. I'd have been better with my old ones and they were bad enough. Maybe Dennis could play it.'

The clarinettist beside him stirred uncomfortably and said, 'Happen I could, Vernon, but not as well as you.'

'*I* can't play it as well as me with these things in. Go on, Dennis, give it a try. Is that all right, Hutch?'

Hutch nodded. 'Right, from the top again.'

The second attempt was successful, with Dennis's solo an adequate if less electrifying substitute for Vernon's. Everyone was happy again.

Frank opened the side exit and stood aside to allow Hutch, Geoff, Norman and Ida out into Albion Street.

'You know,' said Norman, 'if Vernon wore a bowler hat he'd look like Charlie Chaplin from behind.' The others observed their colleague from the doorway and agreed. 'He'll worry about them false teeth of his now, you know. He's always taken life seriously.'

Hutch was watching Vernon approach a group of people. He had stopped and was gesticulating with his walking stick. 'He looks as if he's taking something seriously now,' he said.

Three people had detached themselves from a fourth figure, now almost hidden from view, and were facing Vernon. 'I think he needs company,' said Hutch. 'Come on, lads.'

They set off down Albion Street, the three older men moving as briskly as they could, but because of his age and relative fitness Frank reached the scene well before them.

'What's up, Vernon?' He could see well enough what the problem was, but he reckoned there was no harm in starting some kind of dialogue.

'This lot,' said Vernon, indicating three shaven-headed louts, 'have been tormenting this poor lass.' His voice quivered with anger.

The girl crouched, cowering against the wall. She was West Indian and young, about the same age as Kate. She might have been rather pretty except that she was crying and obviously terrified. Her tormentors were smirking and one of them chewed gum with open-mouthed insolence. Close up, none of them looked particularly fearsome but Frank didn't want Vernon involved, and the others were no younger. He felt his stomach tighten. Out of the corner of his eye he saw two people pass by, trying not to look their way. Cars moved up and down the street, their occupants intent on their own business. He had to take the initiative, and clearly his best option was the low-key one.

'You've had your fun, if that's what it was', he said quietly. 'Why don't you leave her alone now?'

The gum chewer stood his ground while the others looked on. It was just possible that they were a shade apprehensive about this man.

'Come on,' Frank urged as calmly as he could, 'let's call it a day.'

The gum chewer thrust his head forward. 'Are you and your granddad gonna make us?'

'It'd be better if you went. You don't want to make more trouble for yourselves.' He could hear the welcome sound of hurried footsteps behind him. He would have moral support at least. He saw the youth's eyes flicker but the truculence remained.

'Like I said, are you and this old tosser gonna make us?'

The footsteps came to a ragged halt behind Frank. Then a deep voice said, 'They will if they have to, and there's three more here who won't stand idle.' Norman was breathing heavily after his exertion but there could be no doubt about his determination.

The gum came to rest and the three looked around them with affected scorn, making pretence of wondering where the voice had come from, but Frank could sense their unease. Hearing more footsteps behind, he looked back and saw more of the band joining them. He estimated their number at seven or eight. The gum chewer and his friends looked at each other uncertainly.

'Bugger off,' Norman told them. 'Go on, scram!' He waited a few seconds, and seeing no movement, handed Ida's lead to Vernon and took a step forward. 'Listen, we haven't got time to waste on three figures of fun like you, and I'm too big and ugly to be ignored, so I'll tell you just once more – bugger off while you still can!'

Frank, Geoff and Hutch moved in on either side of him and the skinheads treated them to a disdainful stare before turning slowly and moving off.

Geoff bent over the girl and asked, 'Are you all right, lovey?'

She nodded and a tear fell close to his shoe.

'Did they hurt you?'

She shook her head.

'Nay,' said Vernon, 'they were just threatening her and calling her names, but it were bad enough.'

Geoff addressed the girl again. 'What's your name, flower?'

'Ju…lie Wil…son.'

He put his hand to his ear. 'Say again.'

'Julie Wilson,' Frank told him. 'Where do you live, Julie?'

'Carr S-street,' she sobbed.

'Hang about,' said Hutch. 'Carr Street? Are you any relation to Joe Wilson, the builder?'

'He's me… dad.'

'Well I never.' He handed her a white handkerchief from his breast pocket. 'Come on, Julie love. Dry those tears and we'll take you home to your mum and dad.'

Satisfied that the incident was over, the other members of the band began to leave, but Vernon remained. Norman looked at him sternly. 'By heck, little Vernon, I can see we'll have to keep an eye on you in future.'

'Aye well, it makes me mad, that sort o' thing does.'

'Thee and me both, mate. We fought a war to stop buggers like them, and a fat lot of good it seems to have done.'

Geoff was whistling the theme from *The Good, The Bad and The Ugly*.

'Aye,' said Hutch, '*The Magnificent Seven*!' His knowledge of westerns was patchy.

Geoff counted heads. 'There's only five of us.'

'Four-and-a-half,' said Norman, looking down at Vernon.

'What about Ida?'

'All right,' he agreed, 'I'll settle for six. I'm in a good mood.'

Frank walked with Julie. 'Does this kind of thing happen often?' he asked her.

'Some... times.'

'Have you been to the police?'

She nodded, no longer crying but her breath was coming in shudders. 'They just... keep saying... they need names.'

'Does nobody know these yobs?'

'Most of 'em aren't... from round here. They come... in from Bradford and Dewsbury and different places, looking... for trouble.'

'What are they, National Front?'

'I don't... know. That... sort of thing.'

Fifteen minutes later, they retraced their route to the car park.

'He's a nice bloke, Joe Wilson,' Hutch remarked. 'A good builder too. He built our conservatory.'

'He might build you a whole extension now,' said Geoff. 'He's grateful enough.'

'It's not surprising. It was no trouble to us, but just think how he must feel. Little Julie an' all.'

Norman grunted in agreement. 'No trouble at all. Mind you, it's as well it didn't get physical. I wouldn't have minded giving them three a good hiding but I can't do with another brush with the boys in blue. I don't mind so much for myself but I've got Ida to think of.'

'Aye, well,' said Geoff, 'you saw 'em off just the same.'

'It wasn't just me. It was a team effort.'

'Aye.' Geoff considered the irony of the situation. 'A team of elderly widowers.' Remembering Frank, he added, 'And one young bloke.'

'No, Geoff, we're more than that.' Hutch had stopped a few paces behind the others and was studying the street sign on the side of the Exchange building. 'We're still a force to be reckoned with in spite of what's happened to us lately, and what's more, I think we're on the edge of something a bit grand.' He beamed indulgently at Geoff. 'You know,' he said, 'I think I might have found that name you were on about an' all.'

# 5

Frank's sister Penny was impressed. 'The New Albion Dance Orchestra,' she said. 'It sounds official now, ready for business.'

'Yes, there never was an Albion Dance Orchestra, as far as we know, but "New" gives it a touch of optimism.'

'I'm glad the boys have taken to the idea.'

'They're fired up, Penny. The interest was already growing, but this latest thing lit the blue touch paper for all of them. I think they're starting to believe in themselves again.'

'So they should. It takes guts to have a go like that. I'm sure a lot of people would have pretended not to notice.'

'A few did, and I was the one trying the diplomatic approach,' he admitted. 'It was a stand-off until Norman arrived with the cavalry.'

'And you say they've been arrested?'

'Yes, apparently one of the passers-by phoned the police and they found the yobs causing a disturbance in Westgate half an hour later.'

'Good, I'm glad.' Penny returned to the reason for Frank's visit. 'So you want me to design a logo. You'll want it to be art deco, I imagine, like the ballroom? It would be appropriate to the style of the music as well.'

'That sounds excellent.'

Acknowledging his response with a shake of her head, she said, 'It was pretty obvious, Frank. What's the logo going to be used for anyway, music desks?'

He nodded.

'I see. Who's making them for you?'

'A builder called Joe Wilson. He's doing us a cheap job.'

'Him as well? I thought I was the goody around here.'

'His daughter was the victim of the incident.'

'Ah, right.' She thought for a second. 'Have you got a drawing for him to work from?'

'Well, no, that was the next thing I was going to ask you for.'

'I thought it might be. You want art deco desks then. I'll need some dimensions.'

'Fine, I'll see to that.'

'No, Frank, I'm talking about grown-up numbers.' She patted his hand with sisterly good nature. 'Stick to the creative stuff and let others do the sums. I'll come to the Exchange on Sunday and measure the stands.'

'That's great, Penny.' He looked at his watch and stood up. 'Thanks for the tea and everything. I have to catch the six o'clock train.'

'London again?'

'Mm, it's a period drama. We're doing it in four three-hour sessions.'

'You're really building a reputation with those retro scores, aren't you?'

'I hope so.' Work was still thin on the ground but he was always hopeful.

...

'Life certainly had its moments,' said Norman, offering the ginger biscuits around as host on this occasion, 'and as I recall, we seized every moment we could.'

'Who could blame us?' Vernon broke a biscuit in half, considered it for a second and then, remembering the state of his dentures, dipped one half in his tea. 'We were between the devil and the deep blue sea.'

'Now that was a good song,' said Geoff.

'I'm talking about the situation we were in,' Vernon told him patiently. 'Sandwiched between a slump and a war, no wonder we enjoyed ourselves when we could.'

'That's right,' said Geoff, 'and it's not too late to enjoy ourselves again, even if it does amuse the youngsters.'

Vernon frowned. 'What youngsters?'

'My grandsons, to name two. They've been asking me what sort of band it is. They wanted to know if we were Heavy Metal or New Rheumatics or something like that. They seemed to find it amusing but I'm blowed if I can see what's so funny.'

'No,' said Vernon. 'I can't either, but it's not the kids' fault. They've never known quality, so it's not all that surprising if they don't take it seriously when they hear about it.'

'Right enough.' He looked across at Hutch, who was gazing thoughtfully into his tea. 'What's on your mind, Hutch?'

'Only what we've been talking about.' He put his tea down on the occasional table beside his chair and said, 'If I could arrange it, what would you lads say to a proper gig, a dance, like in the old days?'

...

The recording studio was a converted warehouse off Euston Road, and Frank, whose knowledge of acoustics was less than rudimentary, marvelled that such a place functioned as well as it did. He was naturally careful not to voice his amazement, since to do so might offend someone, and the last thing he wanted was to upset the boffins in the tank behind him.

He turned to them and asked, 'Can you give me just a few minutes?'

The voice in his headphones assented so he picked up his stick again and spoke to the orchestra.

'Strings, how about playing the pick-up with an up-bow, but taking the first two full bars in one down-bow with a bit more *portamento*, a real swoop? Dah da *daa*-a dah da *daa*-a.'

'Like this?' The leader tucked his instrument under his chin and demonstrated.

'That's good, but maybe a shade less swoop. It's a fine balance.' Reproducing the sounds of the period was impossible within the constraints of four sessions but he was nevertheless keen for them to get as close to it as they could.

'How about this then?' The leader tried again.

'Well done,' said Frank. 'That's good. OK, let's try the opening titles again.'

The strings followed the leader's example and the effect was as authentic as Frank could reasonably expect. He allowed them to play on, letting them get the feel of the style. Then, as the music led into the opening sequence he cut them off and made the thumbs-up sign to the control box.

'OK, Frank?' The voice came through the headphones around his neck. 'Can we go for a take now?'

'Fine.'

'*Opening Titles and Exhausted Man,*' announced the voice in Frank's ear. He kept his eyes on the video monitor, and through his headphones he heard the click track that would enable him to keep the exact beat. After eight warning clicks he brought the orchestra in.

The opening titles rolled as a man stumbled along a muddy, rutted cart track leading to a farmyard with a wide gate. From time to time he paused to lean helplessly against the fence. The collar and lapels of his army greatcoat all but obscured his face, but it was clear from his laboured movements that he was close to exhaustion. He reached the gate and clung gratefully to it for a few seconds before groping for the latch. His shallow, laboured breathing was marked by tiny clouds of vapour that dissipated briefly despite the stillness, and the effort was tangible as he struggled to unlatch the gate. His toil was rewarded, however, when the iron latch parted with a loud clash. Frank gave the 'cut' sign to the orchestra and waited.

The voice in his ear said, 'Nicely done, Frank.'

The day went remarkably well almost to the end of the afternoon session, when Frank was conducting in free time. The scene called for a slow, expressive tempo and the music editor had agreed to dispense with the click track so as to allow Frank the flexibility he needed. Unfortunately, the scene had come late in the day, when Frank was beginning to find it harder to focus on the score.

'You were just a whisker out, Frank.' The voice from the box was almost apologetic. 'Can we do it once more and then we'll break for the day?'

Frank made a cringing gesture to the orchestra. 'My fault, folks. Sorry.'

They ran the sequence again and he gave it his full concentration. He maintained the slow, insistent beat as the man walked along the passage from the landing and reached for the doorknob. A white, vertical streamer superimposed on to the videotape as a marker appeared to the left of the picture and moved across the screen. As it touched the far side, a disc of white light flashed from the screen as a signal to Frank, and a staccato chord answered his down beat as the bedroom door swung open to reveal the farmer's wife. The beat quickened slightly as the camera cut from her face to the man's and back to hers again before settling into an insistent, compelling pulse during which the two kissed urgently. The strings began their *crescendo* and maintained it until another streamer crossed the screen and a punch of white light signalled Frank to bring in the full orchestra for the final twenty-three seconds of the scene.

'That was great, Frank. OK, thank you, everybody. Tomorrow at nine-thirty, please.'

Frank took off his headphones and added his personal thanks to the orchestra for the day's work. A voice from behind him said, 'Did that scene put you off your stroke, Frank?'

He turned to find Patsy grinning at his shoulder. 'Just a lapse of concentration,' he said. 'My eyes are a bit tired.'

He accepted Patsy's offer of a lift back to his hotel and on arrival ordered tea for them both.

'Tell me about this band of yours,' she said. Her dark hair was shorter than before. She'd had it shingled and she looked as good as ever in jeans and a soft leather jacket.

'There's not much to tell, and it's not my band. I just play with them.'

'It was your idea, wasn't it? You got them started.'

'OK.' Without mentioning the Albion Street Stand-Off, as he had come to think of it, he told her how the players' enthusiasm and self-belief had burgeoned since the first practice. 'It was how some of them made their living before the war,' he said, 'so it's nothing new for them.'

'It would be a shame to let that sort of experience go to waste.'

'I suppose it would. I'd never thought about it before all this happened, but maybe it was pre-ordained in some way.'

They let the waitress put the tea things down, and then Patsy said, 'You'll keep me informed, won't you?'

'Yes, of course. I didn't realise you were so interested.'

'I'd be a poor sort of producer if I didn't take an interest in an unusual story.'

'I suppose you would.' It was something else he'd never thought about, but he wasn't surprised when Patsy trotted out these odd thoughts of hers. It was possible that she'd got where she had by thinking of things that weren't obvious to most people. He resolved to keep her informed in future. Like Penny, she was a source of good ideas, and he welcomed any help that might come his way. It meant that he could concentrate on the musical problems, such as the matter of style that had occurred to him at the beginning of the session.

# 6

'Foxtrots, quicksteps, waltzes and some Latin stuff as well. We've got a gig, Frank. I'll tell you about it later, but can I leave you to sort something out? Penny's here already and she wants a word about the desks.'

'OK, Hutch.'

Frank began sorting through the brown manila folders. There were people upstairs far better qualified to do it but Hutch had given him the job as usual. His best plan was to pull out the ones he knew and then fall back on the most heavily thumbed folders. Some of the labels were faded and he had to screw his eyes up to read them, which was ominous. There had been three cock-ups at the recording studio and they were his fault because he'd missed various markings in the score.

He finished handing out the parts and offered a surprised welcome to his new neighbour, an amiable Welshman, whose name unfortunately escaped him, as names did all too frequently. His embarrassment was cut short, however, when Hutch returned from his discussion with Penny and took his place behind the bandleader's desk.

'I've three things to tell you,' Hutch began. 'The first is that Thomas,' and he indicated Frank's neighbour, 'has come back to us from the breakaways. For what it's worth, he was tired of the sneering remarks one or two people were making about us, so he decided to join us.' He nodded sternly. 'So there you have it. I don't want any silliness.' This was directed principally at Geoff, who seemed surprised at the suggestion. 'I want you to welcome him back.'

There were murmurs of 'Welcome back, Thomas.' Others, unsure of the protocol on such an occasion, broke into applause, like revivalists greeting a repentant sinner.

'Good. The second thing is that Vernon's having a new set of teeth made privately, and I think that shows admirable commitment.' Again, the band applauded enthusiastically.

'The third is that we've got our first gig.'

Frank heard the collective intake of breath around him. Martin Hirst was the first to speak. 'Are we ready for this?'

'We'd better be. Now listen. The Exchange Club are having a social evening on the sixteenth of June. There'll be a disco for the younger end down below, the best place for it, if you ask me, and the proper dancing will be here in the ballroom. They're paying us a small fee, and we'll have to decide later what to do with it, but some of it'll pay for the new music desks, so we won't need that whip-round after all.' His expression relaxed into a grin. 'You might say,' he concluded proudly, 'that The New Albion Dance Orchestra is in business.'

'And we all thought dancing had gone out of fashion,' said Geoff.

'Evidently not. I gather some of them are quite keen. I've no doubt there'll be a lot of members who'll just shuffle around, but they're welcome to do that. The important thing is the gig.'

'We've got some work ahead of us,' said Norman.

'We have,' agreed Hutch, 'and we'll need more than just the Sunday practices, but we'll sort that out later as well. OK, let's get weaving. We'll start with a number that young Frank's found us. "All I Do Is Dream Of You".'

In the corner of his eye Frank could see Penny sketching. She had been hard at work through Hutch's speech, but now and again she lifted her head and looked across to the band with a smile of approval.

The vocal, played as usual by the strings was drawing to its close. He fitted a mute to his trumpet and joined the rest of the brass section as it took up the theme with the kind of verve that was now becoming familiar.

'Very nice,' said Hutch. He handed the stick to Frank. 'Do you mind taking over for a bit? I need to speak to Penny again.'

Frank met the expectant looks of the band. 'I'm not sure I should be the one doing this job,' he said.

'We don't mind,' said Norman. 'We're not a proud lot, and you're a good-looking lad. At least, you would be if you got your hair cut. Mind you,' he cautioned, 'you'd best not get too cocky or we might play what you're conducting, and then there *will* be a problem.' It was an old joke but it put Frank at ease.

...

It soon became apparent that 'taking over for a bit' was Hutch's euphemism for being left with the job, because Frank found himself in front of the band for two extra rehearsals in the week that followed. For his part, Hutch seemed remarkably happy behind his tenor saxophone. Frank raised the matter at a meeting that Thursday evening.

'Who,' he asked, 'is going to stand in front at this dance?'

'You are, of course. You've done all the hard work so it's only fair.'

It was what Frank had feared. 'Hutch, I'm out of my depth. I know you lot can play whether there's anyone in front or not, but it's the rest of it that worries me. I've never hosted a dance in my life.'

'Don't worry. We'll take you through it.'

'You crafty sod. You just want to go back to playing, don't you?'

'That's right.'

The admission took Frank momentarily by surprise. 'Why didn't you say so before?'

'Because you'd have fought shy. You needed to know that everybody was happy with you as leader, and now you know they are. Thomas has seen the light and come back, and that means we've more trumpets than the Household Division, so the brass section can spare you.' He held up his hand to prevent Frank from interrupting. 'Also, you've got the ear and the aptitude for the job. We all know that.'

Heads nodded around him.

'Just a minute. Some of you were playing this stuff,' he said, struggling to identify the necessary calculation, 'well, years before I was born and you still want me to stand in front?'

'About fifteen years,' Hutch confirmed. 'Some more, some less, but that's about it, and the answer's yes, we want you to do it. Any advice we can give is yours for the asking, but you're the boss when we're playing.'

'This is a conspiracy.'

Heads nodded again.

'Listen, Frank,' said Norman, 'I've pulled your leg in the past but I'm telling you now, you've got something a lot of conductors never learn all their lives. You can communicate without saying a word. You make us *want* to play, even more than we did to begin with. Now,' he said, 'don't let it go to your head, but that's why we want you to do the job.'

'You lot are worse than the Mafia.'

Faces beamed at the compliment.

'All right, I'll do it, but you must understand that there'll be times when I can't be around. Unlike most of you I've still got a living to earn, so Hutch'll have to stand in sometimes.'

'That's understood,' said Hutch. It seemed that he was prepared to agree to anything that would get Frank in front of the band.

'Good.'

'Now that's out of the way,' said Hutch, 'we can move on to the music desks. Joe says he might not have all of them made for the sixteenth. There's all the painting to do. Penny's cut a stencil,' he explained. 'It saves lashing out on a sign writer at this stage, and she says she can fill in the gaps so no-one will be any the wiser, but even stencilling takes time.'

Vernon asked, 'Can't we use them as they are for now?'

'No, we can't, but Joe should have maybe half a dozen finished by then.'

'What are we going to do with six?'

'We'll stick 'em on the front row, hide behind them and kid everybody that we've got a lot more.'

'Like Beau Geste did with dead soldiers, but we'll do it with music desks instead,' explained Norman, perhaps unnecessarily.

'That's right. It's not satisfactory but it's the best we can manage at short notice. It's important that we look the part as far as we can.'

'I've been thinking about that,' said Frank.

'Thinking about what, lad?'

'Looking the part.'

'All right, let's hear it.'

'Well, as I see it, a dance band's a much more visual thing than a concert orchestra, and Hutch is right when he says presentation's important. I know some of you grew up doing this, but it was a while ago and old habits fade. I just wonder if any of you know someone who might come in and look at the job with fresh eyes.'

'There's my granddaughter,' said Hutch. 'She teaches at the performance arts college in Beckworth.'

'Little Sarah?'

'You haven't seen her for a while, Geoff.'

'No, I haven't now I think of it. It must be years since I last saw her. What does she teach?'

'Not much nowadays. She used to teach dance but she got promoted and the job's mainly paperwork now. What bit of teaching she does is on the stage management side – lighting and that sort of thing.'

'She sounds like just the person we need.'

'Well then, if you're agreed I'll ask her to come in. I can't promise anything though.' He made a note and then looked up again. 'Is there anything else?'

'Just one thing.' Norman looked almost apologetic.

'Go on then, Norman.'

'Well, I just wondered if our new bandleader might be contemplating a trip to the barber's in the near future. It's nothing personal, Frank, but most of us here are either white-haired or barren, and with that dark mane of yours you're just rubbing it in.'

Frank fingered the ends of his hair, and for the second time that evening bowed to the inevitable. 'All right,' he said, 'I'll have a trim before the sixteenth.'

...

He put down the phone and checked the time. As Penny had reminded him, the film was due to start and she was going to watch it, if only to hear her little brother's music. He switched the set on and opened a can of beer. It hadn't started. They were advertising toothpaste and the jingle wasn't one of his. The next one was though. The advertisement was for Phoebus Holidays. He watched a family in a hire car buzz around a mountainous resort, helpless with unexplained laughter, and there was another silly bit when one of the children in the back dropped his ice cream. It was a terrible advertisement, but if enough children did that at home it might do wonders for Renovit upholstery cleaner, which was also one of his. He listened to the jingle playing out the commercial, thanked providence for gullible viewers and waited for the film to begin.

The music started as a Wellington bomber, back-lit by the dawn sky, touched the runway. It taxied to a halt, which was the cue for the haunting solo by the clarinettist in the mini-skirt. Frank remembered the tiny flower tattooed on her upper thigh. It was difficult not to.

In the score, the sequence was called 'Aircraft Returning and Titles,' and he remembered the music minutely. The clarinet solo faded as a wounded crewman was lowered to the ground, and then the camera cut to the interior of the control tower, where a WAAF with a strong Midlands accent spoke to a tired-looking wing commander. He seemed to have no difficulty in understanding her, which was quite a skill and possibly one of the reasons he was a wing commander. It seemed to Frank that in fifties and sixties films the WAAFs would have been either spurious cockneys or nice gels with Received Pronunciation. A wing commander's job must have been easier in those days.

Although he was seldom complacent about his work, Frank was as pleased as he'd ever been with the score, and it had done his reputation as a composer of period scores no harm at all. He found himself wondering when he was likely to hear from Anvil Productions. Several weeks had passed since Patsy's phone call.

# 7

He hated being late, and wouldn't have been but for the road works in Southgate. He looked around for a parking place and spotted two, possibly the last two remaining. Someone was backing a Fiesta into the far one, and Frank drummed impatiently with his fingers on the wheel. As soon as the Fiesta was parked he reversed quickly into the adjoining space and got out. He locked the door and hurried past the surprised driver of the Fiesta, a young woman. On reaching the steps, though, he remembered the band arrangements, which were still on the back seat. Irritably, he retrieved them and started back once more, and he was at the steps again when it occurred to him that he wasn't sure he'd locked the car, so he stopped to press the remote button. The lights flashed accordingly, so he carried on up the stairs. By the time he reached the ballroom Hutch had started the practice. Frank removed his denim jacket, threw it across the piano and waited for the end of the number.

'Here you are, Frank.' Hutch handed over the stick. 'We thought you'd got lost.'

'Sorry. I'm afraid it's been one of those mornings.'

'Heavy night, was it?'

'No such luck. Can someone give these out?' He handed the arrangements of 'Wonderful One' to Geoff on the front row.

'These are not very different from the originals, except I've given the vocal to Vernon to give the strings a rest. It shouldn't be too much of a burden on your dentures, Vernon.'

'Thanks, lad, I appreciate that.'

'OK then? "Wonderful One".' It was then that he saw the young woman again. She was talking with Hutch behind the band.

He found her in the bar afterwards.

'Sarah,' he said, 'I'm sorry I didn't recognise you this morning. It's been such a long time.'

'Don't worry about it. I didn't recognise you either.' She shook his hand without enthusiasm.

'Can I get you both a drink?'

'They're ordered, Frank,' said Hutch. 'There's one on its way for you as well. Here they are.' He handed Sarah's drink to her and Frank took one of the pints.

'Let's sit down.' Hutch pointed to a table by the door. 'We can have a proper chat.' They sat down and Hutch said, 'It's been a while since you two saw each other. It must have been at Ellie's funeral.'

'That's right,' said Frank.

'Frank's been making a name for himself in television, Sarah.'

'So I've heard.' Her tone was polite, but there was no lightness in her expression. It was as if she wanted to be rid of the conversation, and Frank was relieved when Hutch spoke again.

'I've been talking to Sarah about Saturday night and we think the best plan is for her to come then and see the whole picture.'

'That's right.' She turned to Hutch and asked, 'What kind of gig is it going to be?'

Hutch began explaining and Frank sat back, only half listening. He'd had a fleeting impression of Sarah at Ellie's funeral, but he could remember very little of that time beyond the inevitable grief that was his as well as Hutch's. Prior to that, he could only recall her as a rather fetching little thing. All right, she must have been nine or ten; hardly a tiny tot, but she'd seemed little to him when he was eighteen, and particularly that time she was so upset.

Whatever she'd done in the last twenty years or so, she certainly hadn't lavished much time or effort on her appearance. She'd grown tall, and he was prepared to admit that she might easily be rather attractive if she made an effort with her appearance, but she'd done herself no favours that morning. Her light-brown hair was drawn back tightly into one of those elastic things that sounded like a chocolate bar. He'd seen them often on girls, and until Kate had enlightened him he'd considered it a strange place to keep spare underwear. In all, her appearance couldn't have been more ordinary, and basically he was disappointed. There was no logical reason why she should be a sensation just because she was Hutch's granddaughter, but it had been nice to think of the little girl he'd known growing into glorious womanhood. Instead of that, all he could see was a sweatshirt with the college logo, a pair of shapeless jeans, the scrunchie-thing holding her hair together, and a most unappealing personality. He was disappointed by all those things, but in particular, if he were truly honest, by the fact that she seemed bored with his company before she'd even spoken to him.

She was still talking with Hutch. 'I'll be looking at the overall presentation,' she said, 'layout, organisation, lighting, personal appearance.' She looked directly at Frank and he could see she was eyeing his hair. 'And the general effect. Details are important.'

...

He was still brooding about that when the voice next to him said, '*Anno Domini*, Mr Morrison. That's all it is.'

'Sorry?'

'You've reached that age when your eyesight needs a little help.'

'Oh, is it as bad as that?'

'You'll only have to wear glasses for close work. Your distance vision's fine.'

'That's some consolation, I suppose.'

'Oh come on, it's hardly the end of the world.' The optician was about his age, and for all he knew, might have worn glasses all his life, so it was possibly insensitive to argue with him. All the same, he'd just received the second blow to his vanity in as many days.

The optician handed him the prescription and invited him to take a seat in the dispensing area. There was only one other customer currently choosing frames and she was at least twice his age. Apparently she needed a special pair of glasses for Scrabble, an important feature in her life.

It was all there, waiting for him: Scrabble, Sanatogen, senility... He hadn't properly got the hang of adulthood yet. He wondered what else began with 's' and ended in old age. There was one obvious item and that had been absent from his life for some time.

'Would you like to come and sit at the desk?' The dispensing optician was possibly in her late twenties and she wore glasses. Suddenly he was noticing them everywhere. He took the seat that was offered and his eye fell on a whole wall filled with frames. It was very daunting.

'What sort of frames did you have in mind?'

'I don't know. I've never had to think about it before.'

She studied him for a moment. 'With your hair colouring and complexion we could look at some dark frames, possibly graphite ones. Would you like to try some?'

'Please.' He was a child being led through a grown-up maze. She took a pair from the wall and set them on his nose. He took the hand mirror she offered him, glanced at his reflection and then stared hard.

'What's the matter?'

'Buddy Holly.'

'Who's he?' The young woman looked at him blankly.

'A pop star in the fifties. You wouldn't remember him.'

'No, I don't, but if you don't like them let's try some different ones.' She reached for another pair, but Frank shook his head immediately. 'Hank Marvin,' he said.

'Who?'

'Never mind.'

'OK.' She gave a shrug of acceptance. 'Let's try a different style.' She produced frames of various sizes and shapes, but the original impression stayed with him as in the first waking moments after a bizarre dream.

'The problem,' he explained, 'is my hair. I've worn it like this since the sixties.' He eyed himself again in the hand mirror. 'It's a bit shorter now,' he admitted, 'but the style's much the same.'

'I think it's really nice.' The compliment somehow lacked conviction.

'Thanks, but listen, this is impossible. I could carry on like this and end up completely over the top, like Elton John—'

'I know who he is.'

'Well that's not me, I'm afraid. I'm more the sort of quiet, understated... Look, I've got a hair appointment next. How would it be if I came back after that?'

She looked relieved. 'That's fine. We're open 'til five-thirty.'

He arrived at the hair salon ten minutes early for his appointment. The receptionist crossed out his name and said, 'Yes, Frank, you're down for a trim at four-fifteen.'

'Actually,' he said, 'I think the time's come for something a bit more than a trim.'

...

He swivelled his eyes sideways to look at his profile in the cabinet mirror. His right ear looked bigger than he remembered it, but as he hadn't seen either of them for a long time it was difficult to tell. In a moment it would be safe to look at his reflection full-face again, and then he'd see if they were the same size.

He zipped up his fly, flushed the loo and washed his hands before looking properly in the basin mirror. Yes, his ear lobes were level and they stuck out about the same, but the overall effect was still dramatic. He'd drawn the line at short back and sides: it was less severe than that, definitely more James Garner than Gary Cooper. The only problem was the moustache, which stood out like a lonely bush on a hillside. He tried holding it flat with his fingers whilst he swivelled his head from right to left, keeping his eyes fixed on the mirror, but the effect was still the same. Bravely, he took out his scissors and razor and, for the second time that day, said goodbye to an old friend.

When the deed was done, he put away his razor and, with the rest of his life before him, decided to open a bottle of wine and write to Kate.

He filled a glass, took a sheet of paper from the printer and began.

Dearest Kate,

I thought you'd like to know what's been happening to the band. Actually, so many things have happened lately, it would be impossible to put them all in a letter without causing the postman a grave injury, so I'll tell you about the most important development and fill you in on the rest later.

Writing to Kate was one-way traffic. Like most of her contemporaries she regarded letter writing as one of the amusing eccentricities of old age but, in fairness, she usually responded by phone. He knew she would respond to this letter.

We've got a gig. The boys are raring to go, Maurice and Eddie have come back and we're practising on Tuesday and Thursday nights as well as Sundays. They've made me bandleader, but only so that Hutch can have a blow, the crafty old so-and-so. The gig's a formal dance at the Exchange Club on the sixteenth. It's a pity you can't be here. Penny and Tim are coming.

It had been at Penny's suggestion that they'd dropped the 'Auntie' and 'Uncle', and Frank had gone along with it, but it still felt strange. He took a sip from his glass and carried on with the letter.

Something else has happened as well, and I'm telling you this now so that you won't wet yourself laughing when you see me again. I've had my hair cut – very short. I've got ears again and my collar's exposed at the back. Worse still, I've just shaved off my moustache. The make-over got a standing ovation from the band tonight but no one realised how traumatic it all was for me.

I hope everything's going well for you. I look forward to seeing you again. Call me if you can.

Love you big lots,
Dad XXX

Having folded the letter and put it in an envelope he poured himself another drink and wondered a little about the Sarah character. She couldn't have been cooler with him and he couldn't imagine why, except that a great many women were unfathomable. Possibly there was a parallel universe somewhere, where they were all cheerful and uncomplicated, like Patsy or Penny. They both knew lots of successful people and never seemed to mind how well they got on in life. They were simply bringing the wampum back to the wigwam.

Now that was interesting. According to all the best books, red indians – or Native Americans, as Helen had told him to call them if he really must talk about them – communicated largely in words of two syllables, which made them exactly twice as articulate as some of the people he had to deal with. Even so, they seemed to lead pretty uncomplicated lives, so maybe they'd got it right.

At all events, it was just as well that Sarah was only around to give a one-off piece of advice. Anything more than that would drive him up the wall.

Much more important was Saturday night, the NADO's maiden gig and Frank's first outing as bandleader. As Crazy Horse might have mused on the eve of the Little Bighorn, it could go either way. Frank was inclined to be optimistic.

...

Two days later, he had a phone call from Kate.

'Dad,' she said, 'I'm coming up for the practice on Thursday. I want to be in that gig.'

# 8

When Frank entered the band room he found fifteen seasoned musicians stricken with the kind of nervous excitement they had believed to be long behind them. Typically, Kate seemed calmer than anyone, inspecting her bow for loose hairs and turning the nut minutely to adjust the tension. The others simply fidgeted. Trumpet players fiddled with valves, clarinet and sax players ran their fingers over clicking keys, and trombonists eased their slides back and forth as if their instruments or their hands might seize before they could play a note. Their glib self-confidence in rehearsal was in limbo.

He spoke to Eddie Young, and the pianist slipped out to the piano. Section by section they tuned to his note, checked and adjusted, and then fell silent, looking obediently towards Frank in a way that reminded him of a football or cricket team waiting for a pre-match pep talk. He decided to give them one.

'Forget everything that's gone before,' he said. 'What really matters is that we're sounding good and we're improving all the time. In any case, no one's here to criticise. Remember that people like to be impressed, and that these people in particular have come tonight to enjoy themselves. Let's give them a night to remember!'

Their nods and smiles of agreement made him feel his responsibility all the more keenly as they made their way through the door and up to the stand, but he resisted the urge to follow too soon, remembering that steps were steeper and distances longer for some. Instead, he waited until the footsteps and chair shuffling on the stand had ceased before leaving the band room. He paused in the wings until he was sure the band was ready, and then walked on to the stand, briefly acknowledging the polite applause that came from the tables around the floor. In front of him, the musicians held their instruments poised in readiness, and from between Norman's feet two more eyes watched him intently.

Then they were off. 'Memories of You' would always be associated with the Benny Goodman band, but as Hutch had pointed out, the King of Swing wasn't in a position to object nowadays. Frank thought he might be turning in his grave, however, at the briskness of the tempo. It fairly tripped along, a good opening number for a special occasion. As the final chord sounded with the obligatory tap on the crash cymbal, applause broke out and he turned to acknowledge it before waving the band to its feet. Many of them beamed either with pleasure or relief, Hutch nodded minutely and Kate mouthed 'Yes!'

Frank waved them down and faced the floor. 'Ladies and Gen...' He realised that the microphone was switched off. He flicked the switch and tapped the mike. It was still dead. He would have to manage without it.

'Ladies and Gentlemen, good evening and welcome to the Exchange ballroom.' He ran through a paraphrase of the patter Hutch had given him and announced the first dance, a waltz. The lights dimmed and the band was finally in business.

From time to time he turned to look at the shifting kaleidoscope of evening suits and elegant, colourful ball gowns. The members seemed to be enjoying themselves, openly smiling their approval as they came near the stand, and there could be no doubt about how the players felt. He couldn't remember seeing them so charged up. Even Eddie Young's normally lugubrious expression had relaxed into something approaching a smile.

One number followed another, and in what seemed a short time the band took a break. Frank left the stand first and was in the band room when the others came down talking excitedly.

'Now then, Frank,' said Norman, pouring water into Ida's bowl, 'how are we doing?'

'You sound fine from where I'm standing. The members are enjoying themselves too.'

There was a knock on the door and Hutch went to open it. 'Frank,' he called, 'Penny and Tim are here.'

Penny negotiated her way between groups of excited musicians and hugged Frank. 'They're brilliant! I'm so glad you invited us.' She took a step backward to look at him. 'Mind you, I'd never have recognised you. You look good though, like a real bandleader, and Kate's doing well too.' She drew her in and greeted her in the same way. Tim shook hands with Frank. 'Great, Frank,' he said. 'They sound fantastic. Thanks for inviting us.'

'I'm glad you could come.'

Tim pointed vaguely in the direction of the bandstand. 'I couldn't help noticing the brass lamp holders on those music desks. They are earthed, aren't they?'

'Shut up, Tim,' said Penny, 'unless you're going to tell Frank how much you're enjoying the music.'

'I already have.'

'Honestly, I prepare myself for a romantic evening, I select the slinkiest dress from my wardrobe, I spend hours in front of the mirror, and what does he notice? The rotten lamp holders.'

'I'll have them checked,' Frank told him.

'Not before you've danced with me, you don't. You said Hutch might take over sometimes, didn't you?'

'Who's talking about me?' Hutch appeared beside Tim, who moved sideways to let him into the circle.

'Hutch, you lovely man.' Penny gave him a hug. 'This is a brilliant band you've got here. I knew it would be. Hey listen – you wouldn't consider waving the stick for one number, would you? Just so that Frank can have a dance? Tim's inspecting the equipment.'

'Of course I will. I was going to suggest it.'

'You're truly wonderful.'

'And when I've done that I'll come down and dance with you myself. By the way, Penny, that's a lovely frock. You look a picture in it.'

'Hutch, you're enough to turn a girl's head. Thank you so much.'

She returned her attention to Tim. 'Right, that's settled. Away to your volts, watts and umpires, you ungracious man. I have a partner. Two, in fact, and they're both gentlemen.'

'All right, point taken, and they're *amperes*, Penny, *amps* for short.'

She smiled at him sweetly.

'Norman's gone down to the library, Frank,' said Hutch. 'We need to kick off the second half with a bright band number.'

'What do you have in mind?'

'"Limehouse Blues". It's lively enough, isn't it?'

'It certainly is, but what about Vernon's dentures?'

'He says they're perfect. He was all for taking them out to show me, but I said I'd take his word for it.'

'Who's Vernon?' asked Penny.

'Our hot man on the liquorice stick,' Frank told her. 'Wait 'til you hear him.'

'I'll have to. I've no idea what you're talking about.'

'I'll start the second half,' said Hutch. 'You go off now and get yourself a drink, Frank. Ours are taking so long I think the barley's still growing in the field.'

Frank went with Penny and Tim, who held the door for Sarah and one of the bar staff. They were carrying the drinks for the band. He watched her take them into the band room.

Penny waited for him and asked, 'Who's that you're staring at?'

'Hutch's granddaughter. She's here to advise us on visual presentation and she doesn't like me very much.'

'Why's that?'

'I don't know.'

'Maybe she's playing hard-to-get.'

'No way. It feels more like an everyday case of penis envy.'

'Oh, does it really happen every day?'

'Twice a day in northern climes, I'm told. The days are very long in summer.'

'True. Did you know that, Tim?'

'What?'

'You're still thinking about lamp holders, aren't you? We were discussing penis envy in the Arctic.'

Tim looked nonplussed. 'Who'd want a frozen penis?'

'They have central heating and saunas. I expect they have little cosies too, knitted dutifully by maiden aunts during the long summer evenings, in readiness for winter.'

'I shouldn't be surprised.' Tim stopped at the bar. 'Forgive me for interrupting this travelogue, but what do you two want to drink?'

'Gin and tonic, please.'

'Vodka and tonic, please.'

Tim hailed the barman. 'Drinks for the band, please.'

'Their drinks have gone up, sir.'

'The bandleader's haven't. That's two gin and tonics and a vodka and tonic, all fully fattening with ice and lemon, please.'

They took the drinks back to their table. 'Just in time,' observed Tim. 'The band's coming back.'

Frank sat back with his drink. It would be interesting to hear them from a distance. He watched Bernard Taylor adjust his cymbal stands and take up his sticks. The first number would be fun for him. Vernon was looking perky as well. As Geoff had pointed out earlier, his teeth had been weighing heavily on his mind.

Soon everyone was settled. Hutch came on to enthusiastic applause and the music began. 'Limehouse Blues' was fast and lively. However, the real excitement came with Vernon's solo. He drew himself up majestically to his full five feet four, and Penny whispered, 'Is he the hot man on the liquorice stick?'

Frank nodded.

Vernon launched himself into the clarinet solo with a *bravura* performance that seemed effortless. Few of the audience could see him but they applauded maniacally until Thomas's trumpet entry silenced them again with a high G, which he held for seven bars before the full brass section joined him to restate the theme.

When the applause finally faded Hutch announced a slow foxtrot.

'That's us.' Penny took Frank's hand and let him lead her on to the floor to 'Deep Purple'.

'I'm afraid I'm a bit rusty,' he said.

'Nonsense, you're all right. Move out a bit.'

'No flashy stuff. You promised.'

'I know, but this is a bit minimalist. Let's spread out.'

He lengthened his step and she followed him so that soon they were moving naturally over the floor. She smiled happily. 'You're not so rusty after all. How long ago was it?'

'I was sixteen.'

'Twenty-five years, a whole generation ago.'

He cocked his head sideways and listened. 'The drums are a bit heavy. I must have a word with Bernard.'

'Sh.'

'So is the alto sax.'

She squeezed his shoulder like an admonishing parent. 'They're fine. Just relax and enjoy it.'

Obediently, he let himself enjoy the soothing sound of clarinets blending with saxophones and the soft illumination of the ballroom. It was extreme self-indulgence but he usually did as Penny asked him. It was an old habit.

She smiled up at him when the music ended and they returned to the table. 'Thank you for that,' she said. 'I'm glad I taught you so well.'

'I have to get back. Thanks for coming, you two.'

On his way back to the stand he noticed Sarah helping behind the bar. She looked much better in black trousers and a white blouse but her hair was still tied back. He waved to her and she acknowledged the gesture with a nod and a half-smile but he wasn't concerned. He had to concentrate on the job he was doing, and by the time he reached the stand he'd forgotten about her.

Now feeling more relaxed in his role he was ready to face the floor and meet the smiles of the dancing couples. The whole thing was becoming much more enjoyable. He got a particular kick from seeing Hutch and Penny dance together. In consideration of Hutch's years he'd substituted a slow foxtrot for the quickstep on the programme, and he was pleased to see the old boy make a better job of it than he had himself.

The musicians were having a good time too. Their expressions told him that. They were working hard, but time was probably passing as quickly for them as it was for him.

Eventually he turned to the floor again to wish everyone a good night and to announce the last waltz. There was a spontaneous barrage of applause for the band and they began 'Wonderful One'. Through the crowd he could see Tim and Penny dancing very close. Clearly Tim was on a promise, and Frank was glad someone was, because his company for the rest of the evening would be a collection of elderly musicians, all over-excited and well past their bedtime. Beyond that, life would go on as normal, although there was maybe one little ray of sunshine on the horizon. Patsy had promised to give Anvil Productions a nudge and let him know when the viewing was to happen. Being Patsy, she could phone at any time.

...

He came in a few days later to find the lamp flashing on the answering machine.

'It's not good news,' Patsy's voice said. 'Anvil Productions have taken leave of their senses and gone for a library score. I'm sorry, Frank. That's not all, I'm afraid. The *Hambledown* series has been shelved. I wish I could give you some better news but there doesn't appear to be any.'

## 9

Whoever was pushing the outside door buzzer had no intention of going away. Frank saved his work and went to the intercom.

'Who is it?' Some hours had elapsed since his conversation with Patsy, but the interruption had still come at a bad time.

'Frank, it's Norman. I've got Vernon and Geoff with me and we're not climbing them stairs.'

'What do you want then?'

'We want you to come down here, you daft article. We're off to t' Coach and Horses.'

Frank looked at his watch. It was ten past eight. He hadn't realised it was so late. 'I'm really busy, Norman.' It was a pathetic excuse but he had no time to think of a better one.

'Give over. You can't be too busy to go for a pint with your mates when they've made a special journey.'

Something told Frank that this could be a long argument and one which he had little chance of winning. He hesitated, already feeling guilty about missing the morning's practice. 'OK,' he agreed, 'I'm coming down.'

He found them bunched like carol singers around the doorstep.

'Hutch said you weren't in the best of spirits,' said Norman.

Vernon said uncertainly, 'A business setback, he said.'

'That's not why I missed the practice. I had to take Kate to the station, that's all.'

'Aye,' said Geoff, 'but we thought we'd help you lubricate the problem all the same.'

'Hutch couldn't come,' said Norman as they moved off. 'He's over at Sarah's tonight, so when we said we were calling for you he asked us to fill you in about this morning.'

'What happened?'

'Young Sarah came to see us. It was a useful session but it'll keep 'til we get to the pub.'

They walked the three hundred yards or so to The Coach and Horses, a pub that Frank had not visited for some time. He remembered that it was old-fashioned, as a Victorian pub should be, with mahogany surfaces and wine-red upholstery. It was the kind of place that had scorned the open-plan trend and kept its rooms cosily separate. Unless things had changed in the past two years it was still possible to have a drink and a conversation without having to shout above the din of a juke box or a live rock band.

Ida trotted sedately at Norman's heel until they reached the doorway, where he unhooked her lead. She made straight for the lounge bar.

'That's breeding for you,' said Geoff, opening the door for her. 'No public bar for Ida.'

'Aye, I can't abide uncouth animals. Now then, same as usual?'

'I'll get these,' said Frank.

'You'll get your turn,' Norman told him. 'We're not having you buying a round and then sneaking off home.'

The barmaid saw him and came over.

''Evening, Anthea. Three-and-a-half pints of Sam Smith's, a pint of Tetley's and an ashtray for Ida, please.'

'Right you are, Norman, here's a clean ashtray.' She leaned over the bar. 'Hello, Ida. You're best in here where it's quiet, lovey. The darts team's practising in yonder.' She nodded in the direction of the public bar.

Norman and Frank took the last of the drinks over to the table and found stools. Ida fidgeted impatiently while Norman poured some of the half-pint into the ashtray and set it down for her. Frank watched him, noticing for the first time the liver spots on his hands. It was easy to forget Norman's years.

'That's going down well,' Vernon observed, listening to the lapping sound from under the table.

'It's good for her,' said Norman. 'It helped to calm her down, you know, when I first got her and she was so nervous.'

Geoff looked up from his beer. 'I'm not surprised she was nervous after the time she'd had, poor little scrap.'

'Aye, she had trouble sleeping at first. She kept dozing off and then waking up with a start, terrified.'

Geoff nodded sympathetically. 'So you took her for a pint to help her sleep?'

'Not straight away. She was too timid for that. No, I played to her, softly, just enough to soothe her.'

After a pause to take the information in, Vernon asked, 'What did you play?'

'"You Are My Sunshine".' Norman gave each of them a look that discouraged even the mildest of banter.

'A good choice,' said Geoff. The others signalled their silent agreement.

'Be that as it may,' Norman continued, 'as soon as she was fit I started taking her for a drink and after a while she didn't need anything else: just a gill in an ashtray.' He looked squarely at Frank. 'And a drink'll do you good an' all, so get that pint inside you. The sooner we get you back in harness the better. We've got the branch AGM coming up now our Honorary Auditor's finally got his finger out, and we need to muster all the troops we can.'

Frank picked up his empty glass and made to get up.

'My shout,' said Geoff.

Frank was aware of a conspiracy, but he stayed in his seat and watched Norman take a folded sheet of paper from his inside pocket.

'These are the points Sarah brought up this morning.' Norman put his glasses on and squinted at the first item. 'She was very impressed by the playing. She liked the programme as well. There was a lot of variety and it made people get up and dance. Basically, she thought it was a very successful evening.'

'Did we need her to tell us that?'

'Hang on, Frank. She made some suggestions as well.' He consulted his notes again. 'She feels that sections should be highlighted in some way as they take their choruses.'

'Oddly enough, I agree with her about that, if little else. I don't go for the flashy stuff, standing up by sections, but it needs something.'

'Come on, Frank, whatever you think of her she's trying to help us.'

'Sorry.'

'I should think so.' He moved his finger down the list again. 'Right, she suggests that we highlight the sections with lighting. We've got the lights.'

'Who's going to operate them?'

'Julie Wilson.'

'How did she come into it?'

'She was there with her dad, helping him finish the desks. It seems she always looked after the technical side of things when she was at school, and she offered to do it for us.'

'Good girl.'

Norman nodded. 'Aye, so we've now got a lighting and audio technician. Sarah noticed that the microphone wasn't working. It was a little thing but important nevertheless.'

'Your words or hers?'

'Both. I agree with her.' Norman looked at him over his glasses and Frank refrained from commenting.

'I get the impression you're not right keen on her, Frank,' said Vernon.

'No,' he agreed, 'I'm not carried away.'

Norman eyed him as patiently as he could. 'Tell me to mind my own business if you will, but it must have been very bad news that put you in this frame of mind. What's been happening, Frank?'

Frank was silent for a moment, wondering how serious his problem was going to sound. He was even beginning to ask himself how serious it really was. Eventually he said as matter-of-factly as he could, 'I missed out on a big job that I thought was in the bag. It seems they've gone for a library score to keep the cost down, and it's a bloody stupid idea.'

'How does that work then?'

'It's music that's there for anyone to use – I've written a lot of it myself – and it's cheap all right, but someone else could use the same music for a crap programme about something entirely different and the association would always be there.'

'So why's it there then?'

Frank shrugged dismissively. 'Some directors like to temp-track their films. They patch in various bits of music to give the composer an idea of what they want. It's good for that and documentaries, but not for what this firm's doing.'

After a while, Vernon asked, 'Isn't business too good then?'

'It's not brilliant, considering that another programme that was at the planning stage has just been knocked on the head. It was another period score, the sort of thing I've been trying to make my trademark, and it went against the grain to miss out.' He swirled the beer in the bottom of his glass into a vortex and then drank it down. 'I suppose I'll just have to keep on turning out electronic rubbish for adverts and arranging bloody awful rock ballads until the next job comes up.'

'As I see it,' said Norman, 'it's all in the lap of the gods.'

'You can say that again.'

'I mean you've got to be thankful for the bread-and-butter work.' He looked at Frank a little less sternly and said, 'I remember being in a club in the West End. Bill Cotton was there, and I recall one thing he said that night, because it was so sensible and because he stuck to his own advice throughout his life. He said, "It's no use being clever if you can't afford to eat."' Norman shrugged. 'I just thought I'd tell you about that because it's good advice from a man who lasted longer in the light music business than most. And as for the rest of it, just let me remind you that you're never going to make work happen just by expecting it. That's sad but true, take it from me.'

Faced with incontrovertible common sense, Frank could only grudgingly agree. Seeking an escape from the subject, he asked, 'How did we get on to this anyway?'

'We were talking about young Sarah,' Norman reminded him. 'Give her a chance, lad. She's doing her best for us and she's come up with some good ideas. Oh, Geoff's back.' He leaned to one side to allow room for the bearer of the drinks.

'I got the other half for Ida.' Geoff peered under the table.

'She hasn't finished this one yet,' said Norman. 'At this rate she'll be legless before I get her home, but thanks, Geoff.' He adjusted his glasses. 'Band numbers,' he announced, 'as distinct from dance numbers.'

'What about them?'

'They went down so well it's something that's worth developing.'

'OK, but how often are we going to do this?'

I'm coming to that.' He put the sheet down and smoothed it with both hands. 'There were several members of the Exchange Club committee at the dance, and they enjoyed it so much there's a fair chance of them making it a regular event.'

'Really?'

'I thought you'd be surprised at that. Anyway, more of that later. The thing is we need band items plus a couple of signature tunes. One at the beginning and one at the end.'

'We thought,' said Geoff, 'of starting with "The Sun Has Got His Hat On". It's bright and bouncy and it'll put 'em in the right mood. We need a signing-off number as well.'

'A last waltz?'

'Not necessarily. We can give them a last waltz and then end with say, a slow foxtrot.'

'It sounds as if you've already decided on one.'

'That's right,' said Norman. 'We reckon on "Goodnight, Sweetheart". It used to be a favourite last number in the old days.'

'Fair enough, but I'll have to arrange those two and you know I'm new to all this.'

'You're picking it up fast enough.' Norman fumbled with the flap on his jacket pocket and pulled out two cassette tapes. 'These are from the original recordings by Bert Ambrose and Ray Noble. They'll give you some ideas. What do you say?'

Once again, Frank bowed to the inevitable. After all, it wasn't as if he had work piled high and waiting to be done. 'All right, I'll do it.' He took the tapes.

'Good lad. Now, the next thing is that Sarah thinks we need a vocalist.'

Frank shook his head very definitely. 'She's living in cloud cuckoo land. It means finding a singer who knows the numbers, or at least one who's interested enough to learn them.'

'It's not impossible.'

'Well no, but look, I don't want to offend any of you, but it means somebody of a certain age, and you know singers have a short working life—'

'You're worried about being stuck with somebody with a walking frame and a wobbly voice,' said Geoff, 'and the same thought occurred to us but Sarah's working on it. She has someone in mind.'

'OK.' Frank was resigned. The old boys were gung-ho about things and it was wrong of him to dampen their enthusiasm just because he was feeling sorry for himself. He'd had nothing to eat as well, and three pints of bitter were having a mellowing effect; in fact he was mellowing rapidly. He was glad he'd come, even if it was to a meeting of the Sarah Hutchins fan club, and he was beginning to feel more human than he had all day. It might be a good idea to hear the rest.

'What else have you got on that list, Norman?'

'Another gig. It's nothing classy, just a tea dance at Albion Street School.'

'That's certainly different.'

'It's good. The kiddies have been learning about the war, and they're ending the term with a tea dance for OAPs. They were going to get one of them DJ characters, and then one of the Exchange committee who's a school governor told them about us.'

'It's good for 'em to learn about the war,' said Geoff. 'Most kids I've come across think it happened half a century ago.'

Vernon shook his head in exasperation. 'It did happen half a century ago, you daft old fool. It just doesn't feel that long to you and me.'

'Well, you know what I mean.'

'OK,' said Frank, 'it's a good idea. What else did Sarah have to say?'

Vernon struggled to his feet, fishing for his walking stick. 'I'm going for a Nelson Riddle,' he announced, putting a ten-pound note on the table. 'Somebody get the drinks in.'

'She wanted to know,' said Norman, 'if the pianist always looked so miserable.'

'Poor old Eddie. I hope she didn't say it in his hearing.'

'No, she was talking to Hutch and me afterwards. We explained about him losing his other half last Christmas.'

'Good. I hope you told her he's a bundle of fun compared with how he was when he first came back.'

'Oh aye, she understood all that. Anyway,' he said, taking the ten-pound note and standing up, 'I'm going to get Vernon's round in.'

Geoff drained his glass and waited until Norman was out of earshot. 'Do you mind if I say something, Frank?'

'No, go ahead.'

'Hutch would have been here tonight. He wanted to be, but Sarah had invited him over for his birthday.'

'Oh shit, I'd forgotten it was his birthday.'

'He won't hold it against you. Anyroad, he was torn. You always had a special relationship with him, and Ellie an' all when she was alive, but he couldn't let Sarah down when she'd gone to that trouble.'

'She's his granddaughter, for God's sake. I wouldn't expect him to.'

'Aye, well you mean a lot to him an' all. He was fair suited when we said we'd take you for a pint.'

'He would be.'

'Right, and you've seen Norman look a bit tetchy at you tonight?'

'Once or twice. I know I've been a miserable sod.'

'Yes, you have, and he's not the most patient of individuals, but he's trying as hard as ever he can to bring you out of yourself.'

'I know, Geoff. I'm sorry.'

'What I'm trying to say is, you've got mates who want to cheer you up, but you've got to frame yourself an' all.'

'Yes.' Frank nodded. 'I was just thinking that.'

'Good, and there's something else.'

Frank squirmed, wondering what else he'd done.

'The lads were fired up after Sarah spoke to us this morning. They were full of enthusiasm. Vernon and Norman are the same, and you haven't seen the best side of her yet. She's a nice lass and she can be an entertainment too. You'd be surprised.'

'I certainly would.'

'What I'm saying is, give her a chance, Frank. You've got off to a bad start with her but she's doing a grand job for us.'

'You're right, Geoff.'

'No offence?'

'None at all.' A bollocking from genial, bumbling old Geoff might well come as a surprise but it could never be offensive. 'Thanks for telling me that, Geoff.'

'It's no trouble, lad, but let's change the subject. Norman's coming back.'

'Yes, what's happened to Vernon, by the way? He's been gone ages.'

A voice spoke from behind him. 'I'm here.'

Frank turned to see Vernon, who was now visibly relieved.

'When you get to my age,' he confided, 'you spend a lot of time waiting patiently and reading the maker's name on the earthenware.' He took his place at the table. 'And you think you've got problems, Frank.'

Frank took a pint from Norman and said, 'I hope you lot are going to let me get my round in before closing time.'

'You'll have to do that another time,' said Norman. 'Anthea called Last Orders while I was getting these.'

Frank undressed with some difficulty, leaning against the bedroom wall to remove his trousers because he was unable to stand on one leg. He hadn't realised how little he'd eaten that day until his fourth pint, and then the two untouched halves that had been bought for Ida really found their mark. He let his head sink into the pillow and closed his eyes, no longer able to focus on the worries of the past week. Instead, he found himself drifting towards sleep with the unlikely image of Norman playing his trombone over Ida's basket.

## 10

'Frank, have you a minute?' Hutch was standing with Sarah and a young man he'd not seen before. He looked pleasant as far as Frank could tell, but it was evident from the start that he was very shy.

'This is Daniel, Frank. He's one of Sarah's students.'

Frank offered his hand. 'Glad to meet you, Daniel.'

'I suggested that a vocalist would be a good idea,' said Sarah.

'I heard.'

She nodded. 'Dan's good and he's passionate about the old stuff. Will you give him a try?'

'Of course we will. What do you want to sing, Dan? Is it OK if I call you that?'

Dan fumbled with the catches on his briefcase. 'Yes, that's fine. I've, er, got a few things here.' He pulled out two books of songs and looked nervously for somewhere to put his case. One of the books fell out of his hand.

'Here.' Frank picked it up for him.

'Oh, thanks.' He opened it and found the contents page. 'Is … I mean, what about "I'll String Along With You"? Is that the kind of thing you play?' His hair had fallen over his eyes and he flicked it back nervously.

'It'll do nicely. I'll get Eddie to take you through it on the piano in the band room to warm up.'

'Thanks.'

Frank put his glasses on, still feeling the strangeness of them. He was also aware that the development had not escaped Sarah's notice. He took a quick look at the key signature in Dan's copy. 'Then you can try it with the band if you like. We've got a set of parts in E flat.'

'Whatever you say. I'm easy.' He looked anything but easy. Frank knew all about audition nerves and he felt for him. He called Eddie over and introduced him. 'Take as much time as you need,' he told them.

Sarah waited until they'd gone and said, 'He'll be fine.'

'He's very nervous.'

'He won't be when he starts singing. Trust me.' She set up a microphone and amplifier while Frank gave out the parts for 'The Sun Has Got His Hat On.'

'As it's a signature tune I've kept it short,' he said. 'There are two choruses, a bridge and another chorus. I'll play the piano part 'til Eddie comes back. OK, let's go.' They burst into the opening, and the freshness and boyish enthusiasm took Frank by surprise. He knew straight away that they'd chosen the right number. According to the lyrics, now they'd all be happy. That was clearly the case with the band when they played it, and no audience could help being affected by it. He got up from the piano and heard Norman say, 'I said he could do it.'

'It's not very different from your tape. I made a few adjustments for our line-up.'

'Even so,' said Hutch, looking towards the doorway, 'It sounds pretty good, and judging by the look on Eddie's face

I think we're in for another treat.' Eddie had emerged from the band room with Dan, and it was evident that Hutch's optimism was prompted by the rare grin on the pianist's face.

'Frank,' said Eddie, 'you've got to hear this lad. He's the nearest we're going to get to Sam Costa without a medium.'

Dan examined his shoes in embarrassment.

'Are you ready to sing with us, Dan?' asked Frank.

'Yes, I'm ready when you are.'

'Right, it's a dance band arrangement but don't worry – I'll cue you in.'

'OK.'

Sarah took Dan's arm and squeezed it. 'Go for it, Dan.' She switched on the microphone. Frank waited for Hutch to hand out the parts and then started the number. When the time came he turned to give Dan his cue but he was already at the microphone.

For the second time that morning Frank was taken aback. Dan's voice did have a remarkable resemblance to Sam Costa's; it was as smooth and as warm, but even more importantly he was putting the song across, giving the impression that he meant every word he sang. He even looked the part, singing earnestly into the microphone, his nervousness forgotten for the moment. The band played the instrumental and then Dan came back in on cue, finally putting all the expression he could into the final eight bars.

There was a hush as instruments were put down, and then the band broke into applause.

'Blow me,' said Norman, moderating his language in deference to Sarah, 'How did you learn to sing like that?'

'I just listened to recordings.'

'He's being modest,' said Sarah. 'He's got a big talent.'

'We rather got that impression,' said Norman.

Frank was thinking about further engagements. 'What are you like at learning new songs?'

'OK. I can play the piano a bit, so it's no problem.'

'Hark at this,' said Geoff. 'We've got a singer who can read dots. Lock the doors quick and don't let him out.'

'Aye,' said Norman, 'and if we fall on hard times we can always auction him at Sotheby's.'

Dan looked around in confusion and Sarah said to him, 'Don't worry. When they start ribbing you like this you know you've been accepted.' She turned to Hutch. 'He has been accepted, hasn't he?'

'I should say so. What do you say, Dan? Do you want to sing with us?'

'Oh, yes. I mean, please, I'd really like to.'

'Then it's settled. Let's find something else you know.'


'That,' said Geoff, 'was quite magical. I think we're lucky to have him, and he's not at all what I expected. Not a bit stagey.'

'Not all drama students are stagey,' said Sarah, 'and anyway, I don't encourage it.'

Frank found it difficult to imagine her encouraging anything.

Geoff peered around the lounge and asked, 'Where is he anyway?'

Sarah pointed to the end of the bar where Eddie and Dan were going through the library catalogue. 'They're making a list of songs. You know,' she said, 'I hate having to speak up for him all the time but he won't push himself forward.'

'It doesn't add up,' said Hutch. 'You'd expect a talented lad like him to be full of himself. It's as well that he isn't, but it's still surprising.'

'He needs all the encouragement he can get. He's struggling with the course.'

'Not with his singing, surely,' said Frank.

She gave him a brief glance. 'It's dance where he has a problem. He can tap all right but he falls down in modern and ballet – sometimes literally.'

'Ballet?' Geoff almost choked on his beer.

'It's part of the course, and it's the basis of most forms of dance.'

'Like scales to a musician, I suppose.'

'Give over, Geoff,' said Hutch. 'When do you practise scales?'

'Regularly. At least once a year.'

'More like once a flood.'

'The point is,' said Sarah, 'that they have to be prepared for any kind of audition, anything from *The Boyfriend* to *Starlight Express*.'

'And that calls for roller skating as well,' said Frank.

She looked at him coldly. 'It might amuse some people, but yes, they'd have to learn that too. Work doesn't fall out of the sky for everyone, you know.'

Suddenly Frank was angrier than he'd known himself be for some time. He stood up, leaving his drink untouched on the table. 'I was helping you make your point,' he said, 'but it's your freedom to take it any way you will. You'll have to excuse me. I have things to do.'

The group at the table were suddenly quiet but he resisted the impulse to look back. He knew that if he remained in the building long enough he would risk being collared by Geoff or Hutch. They must have been embarrassed by his departure from the table, but he didn't want to get into a discussion about it. All he wanted for the time being was to get into his car and go home.

...

By mid-afternoon he'd had time to put things into perspective and he was a good deal calmer, although he still found it annoying that the Sarah business bothered him. He had no idea why it should. Compared with other things that were happening it wasn't particularly important. He had no time to dwell on it, however, because just then the phone rang.

'Frank Morrison.'

'Hello, Frank, it's Geoff. Am I interrupting anything?'

'Not really, Geoff. What's on your mind?'

There was a weighty pause and then Geoff said, 'It's about this morning.'

'I thought it might be. Listen, Geoff, I did as you asked. I gave her a chance and she blew it.'

'She's usually so full of fun. What is it between you and her?'

'Search me.'

'You just seem to rub each other up the wrong way.'

'I know, and it beats me. I'm an easy-going sort of bloke and I'll pass the time of day with anyone who's reasonably friendly, but she's anything but friendly. I don't know if it's her time of the month or what.'

'It's possible. Women can be funny that way.'

'But it doesn't explain why I'm her prime target. I can't think of anything I might have done to upset her and I'm not responsible for her bloody cycle either. I think it's just as well her involvement with the band's over.'

'Say again, Frank?'

'She's made her recommendations, which, I have to admit, were very useful, and she's found us that brilliant vocalist. She's done a good job, so now she can piss off and leave me in peace.'

There was another pause, then an in-drawn breath. 'That's not going to happen yet, Frank. She's got the bit between her teeth now, thinking up new ideas all the time, and the lads are game.'

Frank sighed in resignation. 'In that case I've only one option. I'll have to stand down as bandleader.'

'You can't mean that.'

'I do. I've got enough embuggerment in my life without looking for more. I'll speak to Hutch about it.'

'Don't do that, Frank. Leave it a while, at least 'til after the branch AGM.'

'What's so special about the AGM?'

'It could be dicey. It's just a whisper, mind, but... just don't rock the boat yet.'

# 11

Paul Hayden, a horn player with the new orchestra, had been re-elected as chairman of the branch. He would only be called upon to officiate at AGMs and any special meetings, and as there were no other nominations for the office his re-election passed with only polite comment. He exchanged places with the vice-chairman and picked up his copy of the agenda.

'The other office to come up for re-election this year,' he announced, 'is that of Secretary. Only one nomination has been received, and that is Jack Hutchins, proposed by Vernon Waterhouse and seconded by Norman Barraclough.'

From the end of the front row Frank could see the look that passed between two of the new orchestra members. One of them was Nigel Kingsley, the cellist who had been responsible for much of the original ill feeling. Their heads turned only slightly, but the eye contact was there.

'Are there any more nominations?' Paul's voice was bland. The question seemed to be no more than a matter of procedure.

One hand went up. It was one of the new orchestra's second violins.

'Yes, Rosemary?'

'Michael Tattersall,' she said.

Frank realised that he had been holding his breath. He released it in a sigh of disgust. Geoff had warned him and now it was happening. The new orchestra outnumbered the band, so Michael was as good as elected. An angry murmur from the band members confirmed that they had drawn the same conclusion.

Paul ignored the noise. 'Do we have a seconder?'

Nigel Kingsley raised his hand.

'Proposed by Rosemary Bentley, seconded by Nigel Kingsley.' Paul made a note. 'Are there any more nominations?' He looked around the floor. 'No? Then the nominations are Jack Hutchins and Michael Tattersall.' The murmur from the band members grew louder.

'Just a minute,' said Frank. 'This is disgraceful. It's nothing less than a take-over. Hutch has served as secretary for a dozen years or more, to everyone's complete satisfaction, but now the breakaways want to dump him because he's not one of them. This whole thing stinks!'

'He's right.' Geoff was on his feet, supported more audibly than ever by those around him. 'It's as clear as day what they're after. They're trying to take over the whole operation and run it for themselves.'

For the first time the Chairman looked rattled. The noise from the floor had increased, with members of the band and the breakaways trading accusations. Hutch was on his feet, appealing to everyone to calm down.

Paul hit the table with the palm of his hand. 'You're both out of order. It's every member's constitutional right to stand for election. We'll go ahead and take a vote.'

'What's constitutional about a conspiracy? Haven't you people done enough that you want to stick your knife in again?'

Paul struck the table again. 'I've ruled you out of order once, Frank. If there's any more you'll have to explain yourself to the full committee at a later date.'

The noise quickly subsided at the threat, but Frank remained on his feet. 'Do what you bloody well like. I'm disgusted with the lot of you!' His anger was feeding on itself and he was about to say much more when he saw Hutch motion him to sit down. The old man looked remarkably calm.

'Leave it, Frank,' he said. 'The Chairman's right. Let's get on with the voting.'

It was the last thing Frank wanted to do, but such was his relationship with Hutch that he did as the older man asked.

The vote went ahead and after several painful minutes Michael Tattersall was elected by twenty-nine votes to fourteen. Frank seethed quietly through the remainder of the meeting. His only consolation was that Kate wasn't there to witness the humiliation.

'I don't mind losing the job,' said Hutch later. 'It's relieved me of a lot of work, and I've nothing against Michael either. He's a decent enough chap, and he's not a bad conductor for a bank manager.' He took the drink that Frank handed him. 'It's just a rotten shame we had to fall apart like this. As for you, Frank,' he eyed him sternly, 'you must never do that again. You've got your own future to consider, and the last thing you need to do is to queer your pitch with the union.'

Frank took his seat on the far side of the table and collected his thoughts. There could be no stepping down now.

With or without Sarah's co-operation he had to see the job through. The trouble was, it was difficult to see just where the band was going.

Hutch looked through the lounge doorway. 'It seems they've all gone.'

'Aye,' said Norman, 'they've scuttled back to where they belong. And that's another thing. Seventy years this branch has been meeting here, and now they want to move it to...' He scratched his head. 'Where did they say they were moving it to? I was fuming so much about the election I missed it.'

'The High School, where Rosemary Bentley works.'

Norman put his glass down heavily. 'They needn't think I'm going to any more meetings, wherever they are.'

'But we have to,' Hutch insisted. 'If we don't go we're not going to know what's going on, especially about anything that affects us.'

'Well, happen you're right but it goes against the grain.'

'I know, but when you think about it, they're the ones doing the gigs now. All right, they're only playing for the amateur shows but even so, the union's operating for their benefit so I suppose it's understandable them wanting their own people in office.'

'They've written us off all right.' Norman moved his stool to let Eddie Young in. 'Did you hear what Kingsley said about us when he was leaving? He said, "You've got your little band. What more do you want?" Have you heard the patronising bugger play? I can fart more in tune.'

'We know you can,' said Hutch, 'but what worries me now is how it's affected the others. They came back after the first knock, but I hate to think what this'll have done to them.'

'I'll tell you what it's done,' said Eddie. 'I've just been talking to some of the lads, and let me tell you we're seething. All we want to do now is show the buggers. We just need to do something big, something the other lot haven't done.'

Hutch looked at him in surprise. 'Well, I'm glad to hear it. We've got another dance here and the thing at the school, and you never know what else might crop up. What do you think, Frank? You've gone quiet again.'

'He's having one of his deep thinks,' said Norman.

'Be thankful for it. He comes up with some good ideas, especially now his brain's not weighed down with all that hair. Tell us what's on your mind, Frank.'

'I agree that we should aim as high as we can,' said Frank. 'After tonight I want to show them as well, but we've got to be prepared for it. So far, we've done one gig. It was successful, I know, but we've only just started.'

'What are you suggesting?'

'I'm just saying let's not rush into anything. Let's concentrate for now on making the best sound we can, and then we can start looking for opportunities.'

Hutch gathered up the empty glasses and said, 'That makes sense to me, Frank.'

Frank waited for him to check on what everyone was drinking and then went with him to the bar.

Hutch steered him into an empty place away from the others. 'I've been meaning to have a private word,' he said.

'About Sarah?'

The old man nodded. 'I heard her have a go at you on Sunday and I know it wasn't your fault. I've spoken to her about it but I'm blowed if I can get any sense out of her.' He gave the order to the barman and went on. 'She's a bit fragile just now. Personal problems and that sort of thing.'

'I'm sorry to hear that. I'm coping with one myself, now I think of it.'

'I know you are, lad. I just thought I'd tell you. You've both got so much to offer the band and it'd be a shame if you couldn't work together.'

'Well, it beats me. The last time I saw her was at Ellie's funeral and we didn't have much contact then. The time before that was when she was little. Mind you, even then she burst into tears just looking at me.'

Hutch frowned. 'When was that?'

'It was at one of our concerts. It must have been before I went away to college. I saw her looking unhappy so I bought her a drink – an orange squash or something – and she started to cry. Ellie took her home and that was the last I saw of her.'

'Aye, she was staying with Ellie and me about that time. There was trouble at home, you know.'

'I didn't know.'

Hutch paid the barman and Frank started to gather up the drinks. It was one more headache that he could do without. He really wanted to tell Sarah to stay out of his life but he couldn't disappoint Hutch.

'When's Kate coming home?'

The change of subject took him by surprise. Maybe Hutch thought he'd pressed him too hard about Sarah. 'Some time tonight,' he said, 'according to Helen.'

'I thought she might have been back before now.'

'Yes, term ended a couple of weeks ago but she's been deputising for one of the back desk players in the City Philharmonic.'

Hutch whistled. 'Depping already? You must be proud of her, Frank.'

'I am.' He was looking forward to seeing Kate again, but he was also sensitive to Hutch's dilemma. He said, 'I'll see if I can sort something out with Sarah.'

...

He was about to start work the next morning when the phone rang. The call was from Anvil Productions in Birmingham, apologising for the 'hitch' and asking Frank to view the final cut of *The Droitwich Diamond* and to meet the director and music editor to discuss the music cues. It seemed that the library scores had not been too successful and they needed a composer after all.

## 12

'Good afternoon, ladies and gentlemen. On behalf of the New Albion Dance Orchestra, let me welcome you all. We're going to start with a waltz: "I Can Give You the Starlight".'

After a few bars Frank turned his head and looked around the hall. Union Flags hung from the walls between portraits of Churchill and the King and Queen. There were posters bearing wartime slogans, and display shelves had been cleared of the usual team photographs and trophies to make room for tin hats, gas masks and stirrup pumps. The outside windows were even criss-crossed with parcel tape. The children of Albion Street Middle School had taken enthusiastically to their project. They even led the applause at the end of the opening number. The OAPs weren't exactly fighting to take the floor though. They were far too quiet for Frank's peace of mind.

At the end of the number he looked across at Hutch and inclined his head towards the tables. The old man put his tenor sax down but when Frank offered him the stick he waved it aside and stepped down to the floor. 'Carry on, lad,' he urged. 'I'll get things moving.'

With the responsibility unloaded, Frank began 'Run, Rabbit, Run.'

Looking over his shoulder he saw Hutch approach a group of three women. One of them allowed Hutch to lead her on to the floor whilst her friends exchanged amused glances. Geoff, who was *tacet* for several bars nudged Norman and pointed to Hutch on the dance floor. They grinned at each other.

Hutch and his partner were in the centre and he was beckoning to the others. There was a moment's hiatus, during which Frank wondered if the two would have to see the dance out alone, then the friends Hutch's partner had left behind gave their handbags to a neighbour in a wheelchair and took to the floor together. After a few seconds two more couples, two women, then a man and a woman got up and joined the group. Not for the first time, Frank had reason to be grateful to Hutch, and now, satisfied that things were proceeding well, he gave the band his full attention.

'Hey, Little Hen' began to the obvious enjoyment of the dancing couples, and by then the floor was reasonably full. It was a shame about the shortage of men – there were more women dancing together than there were mixed couples – but no one seemed inhibited. At the end they applauded warmly. Frank stepped up to the mike again.

'We've got a real treat for you now. I want you to welcome a young man with a very special talent. His name's Dan Bairstow and he's going to sing "A Nightingale Sang In Berkeley Square".' There was a loud buzz of approval. They'd never heard of Dan, but the song was popular and the pensioners were warming up.

'They just needed a bit of encouragement,' Hutch told Frank at the interval. 'According to the lady I was dancing with this is the best thing to have happened around these parts since the Silver Jubilee. They were a bit stunned. That's all it was.'

Frank felt a hand on his shoulder and realised that someone was trying to attract his attention. 'Excuse me,' the man said, 'what's the name of the young chap who sings?'

'Dan Bairstow. What do you think of him?'

'He's got a lovely voice. Mind you, he's started an argument between the wife and me, not that we ever need an excuse to have one.'

'Is it anything we can help you with?' asked Hutch.

A woman pushed the man impatiently aside. 'There's no argument,' she said. 'I'm right.'

'She always is,' muttered her husband.

'*He* said he reminded him of Sam Browne, and I said, "Does he heck-as-like sound like Sam Browne!" He's got folk mixed up as usual. He does it all the time.'

'And who does he remind you of?'

'Denny Dennis,' she said emphatically. 'I'd recognise that voice anywhere.'

'Go and have a chat with him,' said Hutch. 'See, he's just getting himself a cup of tea over there.' He pointed to the table with the urn.

'Right, we will. Come on, Stan.'

They watched the woman tow her husband in Dan's direction. Shy as ever, Dan seemed surprised to be the object of attention and Frank wondered how Kate was going to react when she eventually met him. He was a good-looking lad and her curiosity was already aroused. It was too bad that she was working at her holiday job all day, but he knew she'd be along to the next practice.

A shrill voice among the tables distracted him.

'I'm not sitting beside him,' an angry woman was saying. 'He fidgets the whole time, and that's not all he does.' She was heading their way, and Frank cringed. 'He lets off,' she told Hutch, as if it were his fault. 'He says he can't help it. He says it's medical. It's diabolical, more like!' She continued on her way.

'There's always an argument when old folk meet to enjoy themselves,' said Hutch. 'I hope somebody shoots me before I get as bad as that.'

'I think they're all from the same home as well,' said Frank.

'But not a very happy home, by the sound of it.'

A deep voice said, 'We all thought romance had blossomed for you when you started dancing.'

Hutch looked round. 'Oh, it's you, Norm. Where've you been?'

'I've just been out to give Ida a drink.' He waved an empty margarine carton.

'I'll take that for you, mister.' A serious-looking boy reached for the carton.

'You're the lad who found it for me, aren't you? Thanks, sonny.'

'It's all right. Why don't you bring your dog inside? We'll look after her.'

'Yes,' said the girl beside him, 'she'll be all right with us.'

Norman smiled and shook his head. 'No, thanks all the same. She's not used to children and she's not feeling well. She's best on her own.'

'Oh.' The expression of dismay came from both children.

'Don't worry, she'll be all right.' He pointed to the posters and exhibits and asked, 'So what sort of thing have you been doing in your lessons?'

'We've been doing about nineteen-forty, writing things and stuff,' the girl told him, 'because it's fifty years ago. We watched some telly programmes an' all, and interviewed people.'

The boy said, 'We went to the Imperial War Museum. They had a special display about Dunkirk.'

'I'd never been to London before,' said the girl. 'I was sick on the coach. It went all down the seat in front.'

'Dunkirk was the best,' said the boy, ignoring her. 'They rescued three hundred and eighty thousand men off the beach.'

The girl lifted her eyes to the ceiling. 'You're such a boffin, Matthew. Trust you to know how many.'

'All right,' said Norman, 'tell me what you know about Dunkirk then.'

'The navy brought all the soldiers back. They say it was a miracle.'

'It was that,' he agreed. 'It was a second chance just when we needed one desperately, and second chances don't come along that often. I'll tell you what. Would you like to hear about another miracle?'

'Yeah, go on.'

'It was only a little one, but a miracle just the same.'

'What's happening?' Another boy pushed in beside Matthew.

'Shut up,' said the girl, 'he's telling us about Dunkirk.'

'No,' said Norman, 'my unit never got to Dunkirk.'

'Why not?'

'Jerry had cut us off. We'd no chance of joining up with the rest so we had to keep going west to stay ahead of the advance. I've never been so tired in all my life. We were all exhausted and hungry. We were angry an' all.'

'What were you mad about?'

'Being mucked about. We felt let down. First we were told we were going to this place, then another place, and before long none of us cared where it was as long as we could stop and have a rest. We'd abandoned our transport some way back when the fuel ran out, and we just wanted to lie down where we were and fall asleep. Anyway, you can imagine how relieved we were when a convoy of Service Corps lorries stopped to pick us up. They were heading for St Nazaire, where a big steamship was waiting to take us home.'

'Where's that then?' Matthew was anxious for detail.

'It's on the west coast of France.'

The boy nodded.

'Well, believe it or not, we were re-routed again, this time to St Malo, and that was where we stopped and jettisoned the lorries in the bay.'

The girl studied his face thoughtfully and Matthew blinked from time to time. Both were completely absorbed in Norman's tale.

'We boarded a fishing boat, and I don't think it could have taken any more of us without capsizing. That's how crowded it was, but it got us to St Helier on the island of Jersey, where a ship was waiting to take us back to England. We found out later that the steamship that was to have taken us from St Nazaire was bombed and sunk with heavy loss of life, so we were glad we missed that one.'

'Wicked.'

'What?'

'Fantastic,' the girl translated.

'What regiment were you in?' asked Matthew, eager as ever for detail.

'The Royal Corps of Signals. At least, that was until we got back to England. I'd lost so many mates by then that I fancied a change, so I transferred to the Coldstream Guards.'

Hutch nodded and then turned and surveyed the hall like a benevolent clergyman. 'Just listen to 'em. They're having the time of their lives now.'

He was interrupted by a determined woman who buttonholed Frank. 'I'm the warden of the British Legion Home,' she told him. 'I hope you're not going to get my residents too excited. They can be very difficult when they're in high spirits.'

'On that note,' said Hutch, I'm going to have a word with the *Herald* reporter before she goes.' He left Frank to reassure the warden.

In the background a familiar voice was saying, 'I'm not sitting with her. You don't know what she was like with them Yanks. If they'd paid her with money instead of stockings she'd have been called a you-know-what, and I don't have to put it any plainer than that!'

Norman winked at Frank. The old folks were enjoying themselves.

The musicians were packing up their instruments. Bernard Taylor folded the last of his drum stands down and said, 'I think that was pretty successful. What do you think, Hutch?'

'I was just thinking about those people from the British Legion Home. After "Hokey Cokey", "Boomps-a-Daisy" and "The Palais Glide" I reckon the warden's going to have her work cut out tonight.'

'Well I don't care,' said Norman abruptly. 'They had a good time, and that's all that matters.' He fastened the catches on his trombone case and stood up. 'I'll see you all on Sunday.'

'That's right.' Hutch picked up his case. 'Can I cadge a lift, Frank? I'm feeling a bit jaded.'

''Course you can. I'm ready now.' He walked out to the car with Frank.

'Norman's a bit edgy,' said Frank. 'The only time I saw him relax was when he was talking to the kids.'

'He only did that to take his mind off things,' said Hutch. 'He's worried about Ida.'

'I gather she's a bit under the weather.'

'She's got a lump underneath. He's taking her to the vet tonight to have it looked at.'

'Oh, hell.' Frank unlocked the car and got in.

'Well, let's not get into a state until we know something definite.' Changing the subject, he said, 'You did a good job today, Frank. That business of getting them started, it's just experience. You'll soon pick it up.'

'I hope so. All the same, I'm glad you were there.'

'Aye well, you're on your own with the next job.'

'Oh?'

'Sunday morning. That's when you need to sort things out with Sarah.'

...

Trying though it was, the Sarah situation was only one of the problems that crowded Frank's mind that evening. The news about Ida was disturbing. Frank knew as well as anyone how much she meant to Norman, and it was a concern that was difficult to dismiss, even for a day or so. Also, the divorce, seldom far from his thoughts, was causing him disquiet. He was told that the *Decree Absolute* should be granted soon if the details could be agreed upon, and although he had no reason to expect Helen to be other than reasonable he hated the idea of negotiating with her. It seemed a cold, impersonal way to end twenty years of marriage, and whilst common sense told him that ending a marriage was at best an essentially cold and impersonal thing to do, he still found it difficult to accept.

Meanwhile, he was trying to work on an arrangement of 'All the Things You Are'. It was Jerome Kern at his very best and it deserved the whole of his attention, so it was unfortunate that concentration had given up the unequal struggle and taken a break. Still, he was a fair man and he conceded that it had served him handsomely that afternoon, so he was more than usually inclined to accept the situation and wait patiently for a resumption of normal service. It sometimes happened quite quickly.

He remembered an open evening at Kate's school, when for some reason Helen had dragged him along to see Mr Baxter the maths teacher, a serious, prematurely-bald young man with a sparse beard. His appearance reminded Frank strongly of Lenin, and it soon became apparent that he was concerned about Kate's future and her chances of survival in the adult world, handicapped as she was by her inability to grasp the principles of algebra. Her latest unsolved problem was set out on the blackboard. It appeared to have something to do with $a$ being equal to $3x - 2y$ with what seemed to be the remainder of the alphabet joining in the chorus. Frank had often wondered why mathematicians didn't leave letters to those who could put them to better use. It would save them a lot of time and, in Mr Baxter's case, a great deal of frustration. For his part, Frank knew where Kate's future lay. She would win a scholarship to one of the major conservatoires, where she would study violin for at least four years, and in all that time she would be required to count nothing more than bars, beats and small change at Last Orders.

But despite such an obvious solution Mr Baxter continued to voice his concern, and it was when he began to explain the logic of differential calculus that Frank's concentration fled. From time to time he was aware of Helen making little noises of agreement and joining in with the head-shaking and disquiet, but his mind was making its own excursions.

He wondered if Lenin had been good at maths, and concluded after some thought that with his serious outlook on life he most likely was. It was possible that the Marxist system itself was based on an algebraic equation, and that was very likely the reason it didn't work: it took no account of people as individuals, and neither did Mr Baxter. Nor, as far as Frank could see, did he value words. If he had, he might have taken the trouble to spell them correctly. Frank had already spotted two errors on the blackboard.

At that point, his concentration saw the light in the window and returned to him.

'What is so difficult about differentiation?' Mr Baxter's question was possibly a rhetorical one but Frank felt inclined to respond all the same.

'I can't begin to understand it,' he said, pointing to the blackboard, 'but I hope you won't be offended if I tell you that it has two f's.'

His observation earned him a sideways kick from Helen and a temporary suspension of conjugal rights, both of which reinforced his long-held conviction that mathematics was bad for his health and emotional well-being as well as his concentration.

And now that he was reconciled to the fact that 'All the Things You Are' was a job for another night, he opened a bottle of wine and pushed a cassette into the player. It was one that he liked particularly, a compilation of recordings by various bands from the early-to-mid nineteen-thirties. He settled down to listen to it, and partway through, a hint of an idea suggested itself to him. He ran the same track five or six times because the idea was slowly beginning to crystallise. Then he listened to several more tracks until he was convinced. After a while, he poured himself another drink and thought about how he was going to put his idea to the band.

# 13

Ida sat between Norman's feet in a plastic collar, like a Victorian doll with a poke bonnet. 'It's to stop her pulling at her stitches,' he told Frank. 'I'll take it off later to let her have a drink. What's that cassette thing for? Are you going to record us?'

Frank smiled at the thought. 'When we make a recording, Norman, it won't be with one of these. I just want to try an experiment this morning. Now, let's get started. I'd like to run through "All I Do is Dream of You."'

Geoff asked, 'Do we really need to practise that? I thought we played it well on Friday.'

'We did, but I want us to play it even better, so let's go.' He started the cassette recorder and let them play the first chorus before cutting them off.

'I'd like you to listen to this,' he said. Encouraged by their curiosity, he took out the tape and inserted the one he'd been listening to the night before. He started it and let it run to the same point at which the band had broken off, just before the middle section.

'Now, what have you noticed?' He looked around the band, noting the same unspoken reaction from each of them. Presently, Hutch asked, 'Wasn't that the tape I lent you?'

'Yes, but now let's listen to our recording.' Frank changed cassettes again and pushed the button.

They listened, and as Frank stopped the tape, Norman said, 'We sound a bit posh.'

'That's right,' said Frank. '"Posh" describes it well. Our playing is clean and more precise but it falls short of their standard.'

'It's a different style of playing altogether,' said Hutch, 'and we've had well-nigh sixty years to notice it but none of us has until now.'

'That's only because styles develop so gradually.' Frank tapped his score. 'Anyway, let's have another go at it and not worry too much about precise articulation.'

They tried it several times with varying results. 'That's why it needs practice,' said Frank. 'We've got to play these things the way they sound best. We're going to practise making all these songs come alive by treating the music as if it means something: by playing the *message*.' He caught sight of Dan standing with Sarah at the back and found the example he needed. 'When Dan sings,' he told them, 'you believe that he means every word. It's as if he's singing to one person and the rest of the world doesn't exist. I'm sorry if I've embarrassed you, Dan, but that's the effect we need to create.' He was also uncomfortably conscious that he was lecturing them but he could see that their full attention was still on him. 'The trouble is,' he went on, 'musicians are far too concerned with technique nowadays and that's why we hear so many of those slick, soulless performances that bore the arse off everyone. At some time in the last sixty years or so musicians sacrificed sincerity for precision, and it's the sincerity that we've got to rediscover.'

...

He caught Sarah before she left the ballroom. 'D'you think we could have a quick word?'

'Certainly.' She looked surprised, even defensive. 'What's the problem?'

'That's just what I've been wondering. Look, can we get a drink and go and sit somewhere?'

She shrugged. 'I suppose so. I was going to get one anyway.'

'Right.' He walked with her down to the bar. Most of the band had collected there already.

'What would you like?'

'Just a slim-line tonic, please.'

He beckoned the stewardess and ordered the drinks. Sarah watched him with a bored expression.

'Would you like to sit down?' He indicated an empty table near the bar.

'OK.' She took a seat at the table and waited for him to bring the drinks.

'I really don't know what I've done to offend you,' he said, 'and I really don't mind if you don't want to tell me.' He paused to give her the option.

She looked down at her drink as if considering her explanation and then said, 'Let's just put it down to chemistry.'

'Fine. What you think about me personally is neither here nor there. The important thing is that we've got to work together. I mean all of us, but if you and I can't get on it makes things difficult. Don't you agree?'

'Of course.' She swished the ice around in her glass for a moment and said, 'As a matter of fact, I was thinking of suggesting a truce.'

'Good.' He was surprised and relieved to hear it. 'That's one unpleasant decision I don't have to make.'

'What do you mean?'

'I was on the point of asking Hutch to take over the stick again, and after the branch meeting it was the last thing I wanted to do.'

'Hutch told me about that,' she said. 'After all the work he's done over the years, I think it stinks.'

Now that she'd relaxed a little she was beginning to look human. If she'd only do something about her hair she might be quite attractive.

He moved aside for Kate, who clearly had something on her mind.

'Dad,' she asked, 'what's the matter with Ida? I was going to ask Norman and then he disappeared.'

'She's had a lump, a growth, removed from her underside. It's being tested but it'll be a few days before the vet gets the result.'

'Oh, no.'

'Well, we don't know anything yet, but Norman's in a state. It wasn't long after Phyllis died that he found Ida, and she's been good company for him.'

Sarah said, 'How did he come to find her?'

'Oh, that's a story in itself.' They were both looking his way and it seemed that they both wanted to hear it, so he began.

'Norman had been doing a gig in Manchester. It was a Gilbert and Sullivan show, *Princess Ida*. Well anyway, he came out of the theatre one night and the first thing he saw was two drunks tormenting a little dog. One of them was kicking her and she was in such a poor state she couldn't run away.'

Kate groaned.

'I'm afraid so, and you know what Norman's like. He grabbed the one who was kicking her and knocked the living daylights out of him. The other one made himself scarce, but Norman was still left with the problem of Ida. She was in a bad way, and as she'd no collar to identify her he put her in his car and went to look for a vet. He had an idea that if he handed her over to the RSPCA they might put her to sleep. I don't know what made him think that, but he got the name of a private vet from them anyway.'

Kate said, 'I can't believe this. It's horrible.'

'I'll skip the rest if you like.'

'No, go on.' She braced herself for the rest of the story.

'OK. Well, the vet found that she was full of pups, which was maybe why she'd been turned loose in the first place. At all events, the pups didn't survive, and it was touch and go with her as well. She'd several broken ribs and she was haemorrhaging inside.'

Sarah sighed in disgust. 'What kind of brute could do a thing like that?'

'We can only wonder. And that's not all. It seems that some busybody saw the commotion outside the pub and took Norman's registration, and he found himself up in court for assault and goodness knows what else.'

'That's ridiculous,' said Sarah. 'He was only defending a helpless animal.'

'That's what Norman's solicitor said in court, and the beak more or less agreed with him, but he couldn't just let it go at that. He had to bind him over to keep the peace. Still, it might have been worse.'

'Do you mean he might have gone to prison?'

'It was always on the cards, but that's all in the past. Let's keep our fingers crossed that Ida's going to be all right. By my reckoning it's her birthday next weekend.'

Sarah asked, 'How do you know it's her birthday?'

'It's not her real birthday, at least as far as we know, but it's the anniversary of the day Norman found her, and that's the date that really matters.'

Hutch fastened his seat belt and watched the row of lights flicker on and off as Frank started the engine. 'This thing's more complicated than Concord. I'm glad I gave up driving when I did.' He gave Frank a sideways look. 'I gather you and Sarah have kissed and made up.'

'Not exactly, but we've come to an agreement.'

'Good lad.'

'Actually, she was quite reasonable about it.'

'Well, that makes me a lot happier.' They drove on in silence and then Hutch asked, 'What was that you said to Norman about making a recording?'

'What? Oh, that. It was just a thought I had.'

'Let's hear it then.'

'I thought it would be a good idea to have a professional demo recording made, that's all.'

'All right, but what would it cost?'

'At London rates, six or seven hundred for the day plus copies of the tape. A provincial studio wouldn't charge quite as much as that.' He drew up at the traffic lights.

'It's a lot of money. We need a decent gig before we can find that much.'

'True.' The light turned green and he moved off. 'It's only a thought. I'm considering all kinds of ways to promote the band.'

Hutch was quiet until they drew up outside his door. 'You know,' he said, 'there's a member of the Exchange Club committee whose son has a studio in Beckworth. He makes demo tapes for rock bands – I believe that's what they call them nowadays – and he might give us a decent discount. It's worth asking.'

'Could he fit us all into his studio?'

'I was thinking in terms of maybe doing it at a gig at the Exchange.'

'That's not a bad idea, Hutch. You can't beat the atmosphere of a live performance.'

'I'll speak to him and see what he says.' He put his hand on the door catch to open it and said, 'It surprises me that Sarah hasn't had a go at singing with the band. She's got a lovely voice.'

'Maybe she'll give it a try one day.' Frank was being polite. With the immediate problem out of the way he wasn't terribly interested in what Sarah might do. He had business in London and there was a chance that he might do the band some good at the same time.

...

Patsy accepted a kiss on each cheek and took her seat. She was as glamorous as ever, and not for the first time Frank caught himself regretting the fact that their business relationship precluded anything else.

They chatted pleasantly for a while, and then Patsy broached the subject that she knew was on Frank's mind.

'I'm afraid the cupboard's still pretty bare, Frank.'

'I'd a feeling you might say that.'

'Well, at least you know where you stand. When something comes up you'll have first refusal.'

'Thanks, Patsy, and I'm grateful for the Anvil job.'

She raised her eyebrows as if she'd just remembered it. 'Oh, yes, how's that going?'

'I've just got the timing sheets. It's going to be a good series.'

'Lots of droll Midlands humour?' She smiled and became serious again. 'I wish I could tell you something more encouraging, Frank, but the only thing on the horizon is so much in the balance that it would be wrong of me to build your hopes up.'

'Don't worry, Patsy. The wolf's not at the door just yet. I've got quite a lot of arranging to do, and you know what they say about being too particular.'

'No, I don't. I bet it's something northern, like "Beggars can't be buggers".'

'I was thinking of "It's no use being clever if you can't afford to eat".'

'Right.' She nodded. 'And that's not northern?'

He shook his head, proud to pass on the information. 'Billy Cotton the bandleader. He was a Londoner.'

'Well I never. And on that subject, how's your band coming on?'

'Remarkably well.'

'You said that with confidence.'

'It's one of the few things I can be confident about just now.'

'I don't know. *Honey for Tea*'s going over like a rocket with the sponsors and the music hasn't gone unnoticed.'

'I'm glad to hear it.'

She took the menu from the waiter and opened it. 'Langoustines,' she remarked. 'There's a thought, and sea bass as well.' After some consideration she closed the menu. 'So you're pretty busy then. This band, is it really good?'

'Yes. The boys have got their confidence back and we've got a superb vocalist. You should hear him.'

They gave their order to the waiter and Frank asked for a bottle of the Muscadet. Patsy was still interested in the band.

'What's next on the agenda?'

'Another dance at the Wool Exchange. After that we're open to offers.'

'The Wool Exchange,' she mused. 'It conjures an image of mill-owners with whiskers and watches and chains.'

'They're not like that any more. There aren't many mill-owners left, and the ones that remain are very switched on. They have to be.'

'It's a shame. Yet another chunk of our heritage is under threat.' Suddenly she smiled again and said, 'It's good that you're helping to keep some of the past alive.'

'Only helping?'

'Thirties nostalgia's riding high just now.'

'That's a comfort. I've been scratching around for ideas about publicity.'

'What have you considered?'

'Not a lot. I'm not very good at that sort of thing. What do you suggest?'

'Let me think.' She began to explore the subject. 'Bus-pass enterprise, music, nostalgia, television… I know a few people up there.' She opened her eyes wider. 'Now there's a thought.'

'Do you think I should approach them?'

She laughed again. 'No way. You're quite right about it not being your thing. You stick to making lovely music and let me make a couple of phone calls.'

## 14

The chug-a-chug, chug-a-chug rhythm wasn't such a good idea. As far as Frank could recall, canal boats made more of a tonk-tonk-tonk noise. He preferred chug-a-chug from a purely musical point of view, but tonk-tonk-tonk had more possibilities as the theme tune for a light-hearted romance set on an inland waterway. Also, chug-a-chug was getting dangerously close to *The African Queen*, and excellent though that score was, it wasn't his.

With that decision made, he experimented with the idea for a while until a pattern began to emerge, and then he was able to sketch the opening sequence and titles. It was a theme that would recur throughout each episode. What he needed now was one that complemented the rural scenery and that he could develop for the serious bit in episode one. However, having spent more than two hours on the score, he decided to take a break and rest his brain. He'd been conscious for a long time, actually since early schooldays, that it didn't function in the same way as other people's. For one thing, it couldn't cope with numbers. He knew people who reckoned up pretty hefty sums without using a calculator or even their fingers, and he'd met people with the most prodigious memories as well. He didn't have that facility either, except where music was concerned, and that was only to be expected. Otherwise he had to make lists all the time to remember the most basic things, especially people's names. There were times also, when he had to make a decision, and it was necessary to list things on paper just to get them in perspective. Still, he was grown-up enough to realise that he had a special talent not shared by everyone, and if he had to work harder than most at making sense of his life, he usually got there eventually. The last general election was a good example.

Helen had regarded his list as a capricious nonsense but she'd never had to make her decision. True to her working-class roots, she'd followed her parents' lead and voted Labour, whereas Frank, who regarded himself as classless, preferred to judge the candidates according to one important criterion.

To Helen's annoyance, he ruled out the Labour Candidate, who described the new Cullington Arts Centre as 'elitist' on the basis that it favoured classical music.

The Conservative Candidate also failed the test because he'd called the Centre 'a frivolous waste of taxpayers' money'.

The Liberal Democrat Candidate described it as 'an example of out-dated isolationist thinking' because it championed local artists, thereby excluding European talent.

At the other end of that spectrum, the Britain Out of Europe Candidate never stood a chance. He owned a factory that made loudspeakers for nightclubs and discos, and therefore bore some of the responsibility for the premature deafness and appalling taste of the rising generation. He'd also called the Arts Centre a meeting place for arty-farty fairies, he'd criticised the length of Frank's hair and prescribed two years in the army for him and his kind.

The Green Party Candidate had never heard of the Arts Centre, but hoped that it had been constructed from renewable materials.

In the end he voted for the Candidate for the Promotion of Regional Produce because:

a. He liked Wensleydale cheese and the local bitter
b. Her son was learning the trombone, and
c. He'd seen her out running and she looked magnificent in shorts.

He was gratified to learn subsequently that she had retained her deposit by a margin of three votes.

The phone rang and he picked it up immediately, hoping it was the call he'd been expecting.

. . .

The news that Ida's growth was benign had spread through the band already, and it was a happier than usual crowd who climbed the stairs to the ballroom that Sunday. Naturally, none was happier than Norman, who stood with Frank at the bottom of the staircase. The latter knelt and stroked Ida's head. 'You've had everybody worried, you little fraud. Here.' He took a mint from his pocket and gave it to her. She demolished it noisily.

'We'd best get up there,' said Norman. We mustn't keep everybody waiting.'

'OK then, let's go.' He reckoned he'd given the others time to prepare.

Norman walked into the ballroom and gaped at the streamers and messages that hung from the walls. Everyone was facing him except Eddie Young, who was at the piano. He struck a chord and the band broke into an enthusiastic rendering of 'Happy Birthday to You.'

Norman took a breath, silent for a moment. Eventually he blinked hard and the words came to him. 'You daft buggers.'

'Now then,' said Hutch, 'everybody's to have a piece of Ida's cake. Young Katie baked it and it looks pretty good to me, so the state of education can't be as bad as the politicians would have us believe.'

When the cake had been distributed he took the floor again. 'That's the first bit of good news dealt with,' he said, 'and Frank's going to tell you the other.' He sat down behind his music desk and let Frank take the rostrum.

'I had a phone call on Wednesday,' Frank told them, 'from the Northern Focus studio. They want to do a little feature about us on the regional news.' He paused to enjoy their stunned expressions. 'They're going to film us here next Saturday at the dance. Hutch has squared it with the Exchange Club, so it's all going ahead. They'll want an interview, and I've suggested Hutch, as he's good at that sort of thing. They may want to interview one or two other members of the band as well. Hutch and I have talked about this, and we both agree that there has to be an official line.' He looked around them to emphasise the importance of what he was going to say. 'There must be no mention of the breakaway orchestra. The story is that we were at a loose end, which is true, and that we decided to form a dance band.'

There was a murmur of excitement, during which Geoff's hand went up. 'What's the problem with mentioning the breakaways?' he asked. 'They were the reason we formed the band, weren't they?'

It's a positive story, Geoff. It's about the revival of the golden age of dance bands, thirties nostalgia and that sort of thing. The TV news people like to end every bulletin on an up-beat note, if you'll excuse the pun, and ours is the kind of story they want. Do you see what I mean?'

'I suppose so, up to a point.'

Hutch tapped him on the shoulder. 'Frank's explained it, Geoff. Now I'm laying it on the line. There must be no mention of the breakaways under any circumstances. Right?'

'Right.'

'Good man.' Hutch patted his shoulder.

Frank continued gratefully. There were times when pragmatism needed reinforcement. 'That's not all,' he went on. 'There's a good chance that we may be included in a documentary. It's about what the older generation's getting up to. There's nothing patronising about it,' he added. 'The message is that age is an artificial barrier, and I think that the programme could help change a few attitudes.'

'It was a useful practice, Hutch,' said Frank. 'We're sounding good.'

'It's just as well. We're going to be recorded on Saturday night.'

'So you managed to fix it up.'

'Aye, the lad was only too pleased to do it for us. It'll make a change for him to record some decent music.'

'It's come at a good time, Hutch. Dan's in excellent voice.'

'He is, but he's worried about Saturday.'

'He'll be fine.'

'No, I don't mean his singing. Sarah will explain.'

Sarah squeezed in beside Hutch.

'What's the problem with Dan's suit?' Hutch asked her.

'Oh that, yes. It looks all wrong. I don't know where he found it, but it's straight out of the sixties.'

'Single-breasted and narrow lapels?'

'That's right. He's just concerned that he might be caught on camera and look wrong for the part.'

'He would,' said Frank. 'Where is he now?'

'At the bar, I think.'

'Can you find him?'

'Yes, I suppose so.' She caught Dan's eye and waved him over. 'What do you have in mind, Frank?'

'I think I may be able to help him.' He ushered them both into the band room, where he slipped his denim jacket off. 'Right, Dan, just try this on, will you?'

Puzzled, Dan took the jacket and put it on.

'How does it feel round the shoulders?'

'Fine.'

'I thought you must be about the same build as me.' He stood back to examine the effect. 'What do you think, Sarah?'

'It's a good fit but the sleeves are a bit long.'

'That's no problem. Right, I think we're in business. I've got a double-breasted dress suit that I don't use any more, so you're welcome to it, Dan.'

'Are you sure?'

'Positive. You'll look the part in it as well.'

'That's fantastic. Thanks, Frank.'

'Don't mention it. We'll get it cleaned and altered for Saturday.'

Sarah looked doubtful. 'Do you think you can get it done in time?'

'Oh yes, if Dan comes over to my place tomorrow afternoon we'll arrange it.'

'Do you know someone who does alterations?'

'Yes, the best in the business.'

'Of course.' She seemed unimpressed. 'They would be.'

For the time being Frank didn't really care. The good news about Ida, the news item and the documentary constituted three good things, and that was how life should be.

## 15

It was time for work again, to concentrate on the bits where the tonk-tonk-tonk-tonk *Allegretto* accelerated to a tonka-tonka-tonka-tonka *Allegro Molto*. He fast-forwarded the video tape as far as the run-up to the action. The Droitwich Diamond was doing a steady hundred and thirty-two crotchets per minute past Ann Hathaway's cottage, or something with a thatched roof anyway, and things were about to happen. This was where the girl with the boat got stuck in the mud and had to be lifted, soaked and therefore translucently attired, into the Droitwich Diamond.

Apparently Shakespeare had many a bust-up with Ann Hathaway, and it offended Frank's sense of justice that the greatest literary genius of all time had to suffer a nagging wife. Even for Frank, that was a thing of the past; his wife and in-laws were no longer around and there was no one else to nag him. Of course, there was pain-in-the-arse Sarah – his last encounter with her sprang illogically to mind – but she didn't count as they weren't in a relationship. Heaven forbid.

He returned to the Droitwich Diamond and its crew, and worked on the tonka-tonka sequence until the doorbell rang.

He found Dan on the doorstep, looking apologetic as usual.

'You said any time after two, Frank.'

'Come inside. Would you like a cup of coffee?'

'Yes please, if you're making one, that is.'

'Seeing as it's you.' He filled the coffee machine and wondered a little about a young man who went about apologising for living. 'I'll get the suit,' he said. He went into the bedroom and took it from his wardrobe.

'There it is.' He laid it on the sofa and unzipped the plastic cover.

Dan ran a finger and thumb over one satin lapel. 'That's fantastic. I feel really awkward about this, Frank.'

'Don't. I was an impoverished student once, and this is between you, Sarah and me. I don't need it and you do, so that's that.'

'I still feel awkward. Miss Hutchins said something about you taking it to a posh tailor to have it altered.'

'Oh, I can see you're in for an education this afternoon. Hang on, I'll see if the coffee's ready.' He went into the kitchen and returned after a couple of minutes with a tray, which he set down on the coffee table. 'Help yourself to milk and sugar.' He took the suit out of its cover and held it up. 'It's mohair, so you'll find it cool to work in.'

'It looks wonderful.' Dan spooned sugar into his coffee in a way that made Frank wish he were young enough not to worry about his weight.

'You'll look fine in it. What kind of tie have you got?'

'It's one of those you fasten at the back.'

'Oh, tut-tut. Don't worry, I'll fix you up. Bring your coffee.' He led the way into his bedroom and found two black ties. He handed one to Dan. 'The easiest way is if we stand side by side in front of the mirror.'

Dan stood beside him, eyeing the unfamiliar tie uncertainly.

'OK, follow me. Right over left and make a knot, then chuck the left half back over your shoulder. Right index finger under the right bit and make a bow shape, then drop the left bit over it. Grasp the bow bit with your left hand and use your right index finger to poke the other bit behind it. Now take the wings, pull them tight and fiddle with them until you've got a neat bow.' He looked at the result. 'Great. Let's do it again.' They practised twice more, and when Dan was confident they finished their coffee.

'It's worth it, Dan. Bing Crosby wouldn't have been found dead in a made-up tie.'

'Really?'

'Trust me, and my old conducting professor used to say that if you wore one of those things your audience would think that either you didn't know any better or you didn't care how you appeared in public.'

'I'd never thought about it.'

'You're not the only one. Are you ready to go?'

'Where are we going?'

'To the posh tailor Miss Hutchins was banging on about.' He took him down to the car.

'Miss Hutchins has been good to me,' Dan told him on the way. 'I've had a few problems with the course but she's been a great support.'

'Yes, I gather so.'

'She just doesn't know you well enough, Frank. That's all it is.'

'If you say so, Dan.'

They left the outskirts of Cullington, and Frank turned on to Bradford Road. He continued until they came to a small development on the left, where he turned in and parked outside a new but modest semi-detached house. 'This is where the posh tailor lives,' he said.

He rang the bell and a small, white-haired woman opened the door. She smiled broadly when she saw him. 'Frank, come in, love. I'll put the kettle on.'

'Hi, Mum.' He kissed her. 'This is Dan, the lad I told you about. He's got a big talent, but he's a bit short in the arm and leg. I told him you'd fix him up.'

## 16

'I'll come to you first, Hutch, and then I'd like to bring in one or two others.' The reporter looked around the band room. 'Who's the girl with the violin?'

'That's Kate, Frank's daughter.'

'Great, let's get her in, and I think you've got a young singer too. Is that right?'

'Dan, yes. We'll find him for you.'

'Terrific.' What about your lighting technician? I think our people will have sorted things out with her by now.'

'Julie?' He called across the room, 'Somebody find Julie.'

She scanned the gathering again and then crouched down excitedly. 'Oh, who've we got here?'

'That's Ida. She goes everywhere with us.'

'Do you mean she goes on the band stand as well?'

'She's never missed a call.'

'Oh, wonderful. Who's her owner?'

Norman stepped forward self-consciously. 'That's me. She sits with me in the brass section.'

'Right. And you are?'

'Norman Barraclough, first trombone,' he told her, like a soldier giving his name and rank.

'That's great. Can we get everyone together? Lovely. Now, Kate, there's nothing to worry about. I'm just going to ask you how you came to be with the band and a little bit about yourself.' She moved along the group, making a note of names, ages and important details. 'Now, it's going to be a three or four-minute item, depending on what else comes in, so I'll just have a quick word with each of you and then we'll get some pictures of the band during the dance. When that starts, ignore the cameras and carry on as normal.'

It felt far from normal, and Frank could feel the cameras panning the ballroom during the opening number. The band was playing well, but he felt more nervous than he had at the first dance back in June.

At the end of the number he turned to speak to the dancers. Dry-mouthed, he got through his welcome. That part was easy enough but the next was sheer horror because, try as he would, he couldn't remember Dan's surname. It had just gone. He broke into a sickly sweat. Hutch was too far away to ask, and he doubted if anyone else would remember it. Dan was always just Dan.

Fighting to control his panic, he improvised. 'I'd like you to welcome a big talent. Here to sing "Stay As Sweet As You Are" is Dan, the Man with the Velvet Voice. Let's give him a big hand!' He turned to the band and mopped his forehead. No one in front of him seemed to have picked up on the omission but he felt sick all the same.

Eight bars into the song his memory returned and he repeated the name to himself until the end of the number, like a child on an errand.

'Dan Bairstow, ladies and gentlemen.' He joined in the applause. 'You'll be hearing him again.'

'What the hell were you thinking of?' Sarah glared at him. 'Do you realise that by the time they've edited that number no one will have heard his name? He'll have missed out on his best chance of publicity, and all because of your overweening ego!'

'I don't know what happened. His name just went out of my mind.'

'It was unforgivable! Were you really so worried that he'd steal some of your precious limelight?'

'I'll apologise to him of course. I don't think there's anything else I can do.'

She pushed past him and left the band room. Somewhere, he could hear Eddie Young talking to Hutch.

'It's going great, Hutch. This is the best thing I ever did. You know, I never thought I'd smile again after last Christmas. How wrong can you be?'

At least someone was happy.

...

Fortunately for Frank, there was no sign of Sarah the next morning and he was able to concentrate on the practice. He'd already apologised to Dan, who was surprised to find himself at the centre of controversy. He'd been so flattered by Frank's description of him that he'd not even noticed the omission. The others were happy enough, talking about the previous evening as if they'd been making television programmes all their lives but even so, Frank wondered how many of them were counting the hours to Monday's regional news. He was dreading it.

He gave Kate a lift home, and when he stopped outside the house, she asked, 'Are you coming in?'

He hadn't intended to, but he couldn't see any harm in having a quick word with Helen. He found her in the kitchen.

'Hello, I didn't expect to see you.' She appeared flushed, as if she'd been caught out in some way.

'I just thought I'd make a flying visit.'

'Fine, I'll put the kettle on. How are things?'

'So-so. How are your things?'

'Mustn't grumble.'

'I don't think I can cope with the pace of this conversation,' said Kate. 'I'm going up to my room.' She closed the kitchen door behind her.

'Maybe I should go,' he suggested. 'Kate's still uncomfortable.'

'No.' She waved him down. 'Don't go yet. Sit down for a minute.' She was clearly flustered. 'I was going to phone you anyway.'

'Were you?' He could see that she was psyching herself up to say something important. She'd looked much the same the night she told him she wanted the divorce.

Eventually she said, 'I'm seeing someone. Kate doesn't know yet. I'm going to tell her when you've gone.' She was examining the nails of her right hand.

'I see.' He'd been half-expecting it. It had just come a lot sooner than he'd anticipated. 'I don't understand,' he said. 'I mean, if Kate knows nothing about it, when has this been happening?'

'We've been seeing each other at odd times, mainly when Kate was away. It began about two months ago.

He nodded slowly, still stunned.

'Aren't you going to say anything?'

'There's nothing to say.'

She continued to inspect her nails. 'His name's Robert,' she said, as if it were important for him to have the information, 'and he has two teenage boys.'

'It serves him right.'

Ignoring the remark, she went on. 'He's a civil servant.'

'What kind?' In Frank's experience, civil servants came in two categories: those that relieved him of money and those that didn't, and even in his current state of shock the distinction was important.

'He works in the Finance Department...' She held up a hand to forestall any comment. 'He doesn't agree with the Community Charge either but he has to follow orders.'

It seemed that Helen was doing her share of conforming too. Like everyone else he knew, she'd always referred to it as the Poll Tax.

'That was Eichmann's defence.'

'What was?'

'That he was only obeying orders.'

'Now you're being petty, Frank. I'm telling you about him so that it's all out in the open, but you're not making it at all easy for me.'

'I don't see why I should.'

She bit her lip and said, 'I think you'd better go now. I need to talk to Kate.'

He was angry and confused. Their marriage had been effectively over for more than a year. He'd settled for that, so why did it bother him that his wife was having a relationship with someone else? Why did it hurt when he thought of them together? It was as if, after twenty years of marriage, he needed another twenty to get her properly out of his system. He knew it was ridiculous, but certainly something inside him was reluctant to let go.

Presumably this bloke's two boys had been as ignorant of what was happening as Kate was. He knew nothing about them, but it was anybody's guess how Kate would react. She'd been remarkably philosophical about the situation so far, but this was different. He half-expected her to arrive at his door at any moment.

He contained himself until ten-past four, by which time he felt sure Helen must have told her. He hesitated and then dialled the number, no longer caring about what Helen might say. After a second's delay the engaged tone sounded. He swore. No doubt she was talking to lover boy, telling him that it was out in the open and they could do what the hell they liked. He waited several minutes and tried again. It was still engaged.

The light was flashing on the answer phone and he remembered that there was a message from Hutch asking him to ring back. He hoped it wasn't about bloody Sarah, because he was sick of hearing her name, but he dialled Hutch's number anyway. It was something to do.

Hutch answered straight away.

'Hello, Frank. I'm afraid it's bad news. Eddie Young collapsed this morning. It happened soon after you left.'

It was the last thing Frank had expected. 'What was it, a heart attack?'

'A stroke, we think. One minute he was chatting and laughing with the rest of us, and the next he was face down on the bar. They've taken him to Cullington General.'

## 17

'To hell with it.' Norman was in a philosophical mood. 'Life's too short. If you want a pint, have a pint. If you want a bit of a flutter on the horses, have one and enjoy yourself, I say. A short life and a gay one, and I mean that in the old-fashioned sense, of course.'

They were gathered in the Exchange Club lounge to watch the news item on the large-screen TV but the occasion was inevitably overshadowed by Eddie's collapse.

'It makes you think,' said Geoff. 'We're nearly all at that sort of age. It could happen to any of us.'

'It's being so cheerful that keeps him going,' said Vernon.

'Well, it's a shock,' said Geoff. 'Poor old Eddie had just started to live again after Dorothy's death, and all of a sudden down he went. There's no justice.'

'Don't write him off,' Vernon protested, 'he's not dead yet.'

Norman grunted. 'He might as well be, unconscious and fed through plastic plumbing. I hope somebody shoots me before I get to that stage.'

Hutch sat beside Frank and touched his arm. 'No Katie tonight?'

'No.'

'Trouble?'

Frank nodded. 'I'll tell you about it later.'

'OK, lad. It'll be a shame if she misses this.'

'I've set the video at home.'

'Good thinking. I hope they're going to show it tonight. They seem to be taking forever.'

'There's time, Hutch. They haven't got through the main news yet.'

The bulletin continued. There seemed to be very little that was newsworthy. Frank gripped the arms of his chair, wishing they'd go on to the item and end his suspense.

'Are you still kicking yourself about Saturday night?'

Frank nodded tensely. 'I phoned the studio this morning. It took ages for me to speak to someone with some clout.'

'Did you get anywhere?'

'I don't know. They said they'd do what they could, but you know how it works. They've got other things to think about.'

'It was a natural thing to happen, Frank, and you did well to come up with that "Velvet Voice" stuff. That's what they used to call Jack Plant in the old days, you know.'

Frank was not in the mood for reminiscing. 'I don't give a damn about myself, Hutch,' he said. This isn't how I make my living.'

'I know. You're feeling it on our account. You've carried this band on your back from the start.' He leaned sideways confidentially and said, 'I've given Sarah a piece of my mind. It was overdue.'

'Hush!' said Vernon. 'They're coming to it.'

In the newsroom Brian Anderson shuffled his papers and smiled into the camera. All eyes were on the screen.

'Retirement is the time to sit back and take things easy,' he was saying. 'Maybe to enjoy a round of golf or potter about the garden. At least, that's the popular idea, but we've heard about a group of pensioners who are taking life anything but easy. They're the New Albion Dance Orchestra, based in Cullington, and Kirstie Edwards went to the Wool Exchange there to meet them.'

There was a cut to the ballroom. The reporter was standing beside the bar and behind her the dance was already in progress.

'I'm in the ballroom at Cullington Wool Exchange,' she said. 'There's a fantastic atmosphere here and it's all been brought about by the band you can hear behind me.'

Frank was completely thrown. They were playing 'Lovely Lady'. It was the waltz they'd played after Dan's first number.

'This is the New Albion Dance Orchestra, which consists largely of retired musicians. They were formed only three months ago, and since then they've been recreating the wonderful, romantic sounds of the nineteen-thirties. I spoke to some of them earlier.' There was another cut to the band room.

'Now, Jack Hutchins, known to everyone as "Hutch", I believe you play a co-ordinating role with the band. Tell me how it all started.'

'It was Frank, our bandleader as he is now, who came up with the idea of forming a dance band. Some of us had played with bands in the past, and it seemed like a good idea.'

'Right, so you've all been professional musicians?'

'That's right.' He indicated his neighbour. 'Norman here played in the ballroom of the SS Duchess of Lancaster before he joined me in London, and Vernon, our First Reed played in the West End as well.'

'So let's have a word with Norman Barraclough, First Trombonist.' She took the microphone to Norman. 'Tell me, how does it feel to be playing this music again after so many years?'

Norman approached the microphone self-consciously. 'That's the best part about it,' he said. 'We start playing and it's as if the years have rolled away. The music's the same. There's just more white hair about than there was in the old days.'

Frank groaned when he saw himself on the screen.

'Frank Morrison, you're the leader of the band and it was your idea. Tell me, what made you think of it?'

'It was the obvious thing to do. There was a lot of talent going to waste and something had to be done. We had the right instruments and the players with the right background, so we just had to form a band.'

'You're considerably younger than most of the players, aren't you?'

'Yes, I'm a youngster of forty-one, so I rely a lot on the experience of the older members.'

He listened to himself and cringed. If only she would move on to Dan.

'Some of the band are even younger,' said Kirstie. 'This is Kate, who's nineteen, and Julie's eighteen.' She asked them how it felt to be working with people two generations older, and how they felt about the music. They answered well, considering they must have felt as intimidated as anyone by the cameras.

'Now, one very important member of the band is resident vocalist Dan Bairstow.'

Frank expelled an audible sigh of relief.

'Dan, how did you come to be singing with the band? It's unusual for a chap of your age, isn't it?'

Hesitating with shyness and stage nerves, Dan replied, mentioning that he'd been introduced to the band by his college tutor, and that the kind of music he was singing was very special to him. He came across as he always did, with transparent sincerity, and Frank felt sufficiently recovered to enjoy the final part of the interview.

'Before we hear the band again,' said Kirstie, 'there's one more member I'd like you to meet.' The camera cut to Ida, who was sitting watchful as usual beside Norman's mirror-polished shoes. Kirstie crouched down and stroked her. 'Her name's Ida and her place is in the brass section with Norman here. He tells me Ida wasn't very well recently, but in spite of that she never missed a band call.' She stroked her again and straightened up, smiling to the camera. 'Before we leave the Cullington Wool Exchange, let's hear some more of this wonderful music.'

Dan was singing "Love is the Sweetest Thing". There was a close-up of him, then each section of the band, and finally they zoomed in on Ida, who was watching the camera very carefully.

Back in the studio Elaine Roper said, 'What a wonderful sound, and what a voice that singer's got! What's his name again?'

'Dan Bairstow. Apparently the bandleader's dubbed Dan "The Man with the Velvet Voice."'

'I like that.'

'Me too.' Brian faced the camera again and said, 'And now for a look at tomorrow's weather.'

The band members, who had been largely silent during the item, began to speak at once.

'First class,' said Bernard Taylor. 'They've done us proud.'

'It was a good thing Norman polished his shoes,' said Geoff.

'I polish 'em every night, you cheeky devil.'

'Who'd have thought, three months ago,' said Martin Hirst, 'that we'd be on the box?'

'If it comes to that,' asked Vernon, 'who'd have thought we'd still be playing? It's all down to young Frank. Where is he?'

'He's here beside me,' Hutch told him. 'He's recovering from palpitations. Are you all right, Frank?'

'I am now.' His heart was still pounding but his conscience was clear.

'Aye, you can relax. They didn't show your cock-up after all—' Suddenly Hutch was distracted. 'I think we're about to receive a deputation,' he said. The others were all looking towards them.

'We've been talking,' said Norman. 'What we're wondering is, where are we going to find another pianist now Eddie's laid low?'

'I suppose I'll have to fill in again,' said Fred Adams.

'You could sound a bit more enthusiastic.'

'How would you feel if you turned up to play your trombone and they put you on the triangle?'

'Wait a minute, all of you.' Hutch held out his hands for silence. 'Poor old Martin's trying to make his voice heard and it's impossible above you lot. What is it, Martin?'

Martin Hirst took his hand down gratefully. 'I know someone who might do it, Hutch,' he said. 'She's classically trained, at the Academy, but she can turn her hand to anything. It's just a question of persuading her to come along to a practice.'

# 18

It was a bigger Tuesday post than usual and instead of flipping through the envelopes as he picked them up Frank took them to the flat, where he dropped them on his studio desk. He discarded the inevitable fliers advertising credit cards, insurance and private health care, and opened an envelope which he knew contained his private bank statement. He seldom gave it more than a cursory glance, financial matters being better left to those qualified to deal with them, but on this occasion one item met his eye immediately. It was his monthly direct debit to the Metropolitan Council Finance Department.

Now that was cruel, and it was also a reminder by loose association, as if such a thing were needed, that he had to speak to Kate. Helen's phone had been giving the engaged tone for so long that he'd even had the engineers check the line.

He needed to finish the score, which would take about two hours. He also needed bread, milk and coffee urgently. Without the coffee he couldn't possibly finish the score, so the decision was made. He would go to the supermarket where Britannia Mills used to be – he could never remember its name – and on the way he would call on Kate at work.

He parked in the supermarket car park and walked through the covered alley that led into Northgate, almost opposite The Copper Kettle.

The place was empty except for a young waitress, who came to take his order.

'Coffee, please.'

'A cafetiére?'

'No, just a cup. Is Kate working today?' He saw her hesitate. 'I'm her dad,' he assured her.

'Oh, right. Yes, I'll tell her you're here.'

After a few seconds Kate brought his coffee. She looked grey and short on sleep. 'Dad,' she said, 'what are you doing here?'

'I've come to see you. I couldn't get through on the phone.'

She shifted uncomfortably.

'Are you all right? That's what I wanted to know. I mean, if you want to talk or anything—'

'Don't worry about me, Dad. Just look after yourself.'

'But I do worry about you, so come to the flat. I'll square it with your mum.' She looked so miserable he wanted to take her in his arms and hug her. Instead, he spared her embarrassment and squeezed her hand. 'Just pack a bag and come over after work.'

She nodded, biting her lip.

'Is there a phone here that I can use?'

She led him to a wall phone beside the kitchen door before leaving him in order to serve two new customers.

He dialled the library's number.

'Cullington Public Library.' It was Helen's voice.

'Helen—'

'We're busy, Frank. What do you want?'

'I'm busy too. Is that how you greet your punters?'

Her voice was cold. 'We don't have punters, we have readers and borrowers.'

'Good. In that case I want to borrow my daughter for an indefinite period.'

'You want her to stay with you?'

'That's right. Of course, it's her freedom where she goes, but I thought I'd let you know out of courtesy.'

'That's big of you.'

He could hear her tapping with her pencil. It was her equivalent of making a decision list. Eventually she said, 'As you say, it's up to her, and maybe she needs a change of scenery.'

'Yes, maybe she does.' Unable to conceal his anger for much longer he put down the receiver and left.

So Kate needed a change of scenery. That wasn't surprising, and neither was Helen's compliance, albeit after a token hesitation. It would give her a clear run with the new man in her life. He imagined the interloper to be prematurely middle-aged, with dark-rimmed glasses and a serious approach to life, and the picture might have amused him at one time but the thought of them together was too awful.

He collected a basket on the way into the supermarket. Milk and bread were on the far side and coffee was halfway down. He got the bread and milk first and was scanning the coffee shelves for the beans he wanted, when he heard a familiar voice.

'Hello, Frank.' The voice was Sarah's, and for once she looked remarkably friendly.

'Oh, hello.' He continued to search the shelves for coffee beans. He wasn't going to rush into conversation.

'I'm doing the weekly shop for Hutch,' she said. 'I do it when I can, now he doesn't drive any more.'

'That's very generous of you. Ah, there it is.' He spotted the label and took a packet from the top shelf. He had the impression that she was making conversation, in which case she would have to try harder.

'I'm glad I bumped into you. I want to thank you for phoning the TV studio. Hutch told me.'

'I didn't do it for your benefit.' He dropped the coffee casually into his basket. It felt good, giving her the cold shoulder. He was improving.

'I realise that.' She bit her lip. 'I'm afraid I over-reacted on Saturday night.'

'I won't argue with that.'

'No, I suppose not.' She seemed unusually deflated. 'Frank, I'd really like to talk, but not here. Are you very busy right now?'

'With work that dropped out of the sky or the kind I had to pull the usual way?'

She winced. 'I shouldn't have said that either.'

'That's right. What do you want to talk about?'

'Look, can we go somewhere a bit less public? It's difficult here.'

'I've got work waiting to be done, but five minutes won't make much difference. There's the cafeteria here.'

'Fine. I've got what I need. I'll wait for you.'

'No, I'm finished now.'

After a short time they both emerged from the checkout and headed for the cafeteria bar.

'What would you like?' she asked. Coffee? I'll get them.'

'Yes please, coffee's fine. I'll get a tray.' While Sarah was getting the coffee, he picked up some miniature cartons of cream, some sachets of sugar and a couple of plastic teaspoons.

'Where shall we sit? Is this one OK?' She stopped by a small table near the entrance.

'Fine by me.'

She poured cream into her cup and stirred it, wrinkling her nose as she did so. 'The coffee doesn't get any better,' she remarked.

'I wouldn't know,' he said. 'I've never been in here before.'

She looked down, nervously tracing an imaginary circle on the table with her forefinger and said, 'You're not making this easy.'

Helen had said that, and it made him no less angry that Sarah was accusing him of the same thing. 'I've been as polite to you as I can be,' he told her, 'because you're Hutch's granddaughter and he's my oldest and closest friend. I also made a pact with you. If you remember, we agreed to bury whatever differences you thought we had, and then on Saturday night I realised I'd been wasting my breath. Now, it seems, you want me to make things easy for you.'

'I know. I've been impossible and I'm sorry.'

'That'll do for a start.'

'Right, will you let me explain first of all, why I'm so protective towards Dan?'

'Be my guest.'

She stirred her coffee again unnecessarily. 'He came from the most disadvantaged background, both socially and financially but he's got a terrific talent. I was at his audition and I realised that immediately. He's got his problems with certain forms of dance, but I was prepared to do extra work with him to bring him up to scratch. I really want him to succeed. He's had a rotten start in life, and he deserves to do well.' She tasted her coffee again and pushed it aside. 'I suppose I'm speaking a foreign language as far as you're concerned.'

'You may well believe that but you're wrong. I wasn't born with an investment portfolio in my sticky little hand. I don't know why I'm telling you this, unless it's because I'm sick of being resented for what success I've had, but I went to the Royal College of Music on a scholarship that I won. I also worked bloody hard for extra money. It wasn't easy for my mother to keep my sister and me at school and then let us go to college but it's very much to her credit that she did.'

'I didn't realise that.'

'I can't imagine you did.' He sipped some of his coffee and grimaced. It would help him appreciate the stuff he'd just bought. 'I don't know what problems Dan's had, and I'm not going to pry, but my father died when I was three so I remember very little about him. The point is that my mother was left with two of us to bring up, and she did it by taking in dressmaking and alterations. She made wedding cakes as well, as I remember.'

'Oh hell, Frank, I'm sorry.'

'All right, but I still don't understand why you resent me as much as you do, unless you're a Marxist or something of that kind.'

'No, I'm not. I'm not interested in politics.'

'So we agree on one thing at least.'

'I hope so.' She finished examining her plastic teaspoon and bent it in half. 'When Hutch asked me to come to that band practice he told me I'd be seeing an old friend. He told me you were leading the band. I remembered you, of course, and I thought it would be pleasant to see you again after all that time.'

'It obviously wasn't.'

'Well, the first I saw of you was in the car park, drumming your fingers impatiently while you waited for me to park. You dashed past me and then came back for something, and with a flamboyant gesture you locked the doors on your big, expensive car and ignored me again on the way up to the ballroom. It wasn't a good start.'

'Maybe not. I was late, and to make matters worse, I'd left the arrangements I'd done for the band in my car, which, incidentally, is a Saab, not a Bentley, and being muddle-headed I forgot to lock it. I didn't recognise you because the last time I'd seen you was at Ellie's funeral, when you were wearing a black dress and hat.'

'Hell.' She let her eyelids fall shut.

'You didn't help matters by taking a swipe at my hair.'

'I know. I was surprised when you had it cut short.'

'So was I, but that's another story. Suffice it to say I didn't have it cut because you disapproved of it, or to change my image, whatever that is.'

'I'm glad.'

'Do you spend your life jumping to conclusions about people?'

'Not usually.'

'You just reserve the treatment for me.' He was aware that two elderly people at the next table were watching him with a degree of hostility. He wondered for a moment what they were thinking.

'I'm sorry.' She sounded completely dejected. 'I've made a fool of myself. I think I'd better go.'

He'd gone further than he'd intended. The old boy at the next table was almost on his feet, ready to come to her defence.

'No, don't,' he said. 'I think we're actually getting somewhere this time.'

'I can't blame you for being angry.'

He looked at the lukewarm coffee and decided to leave it. 'Maybe I'm a shade touchy from time to time. It's not my practice to make excuses, but the fact is that my wife told me recently that she'd taken up with an amorous tax collector. OK, the marriage has been over for more than a year now, but it's my daughter I worry about. She's taken everything incredibly well up to now, but I really don't know how she's coping with this latest development.'

She lowered her eyes. 'I know,' she said, 'Kate told me about it.'

'She told you? When was this?'

'She phoned me on Sunday. She was terribly upset.'

'I didn't know she talked to you.'

'She does sometimes. I think it's because I'm closer to her in age than most people she knows, apart from her friends in London, that is.'

'Well,' he mused, 'life is full of surprises.'

'Are you angry?'

'Not really, just surprised.'

'I never criticised you to her. You needn't worry about that.'

'I shan't.'

'It was a long phone call and it wasn't the only one. Your wife won't be pleased when she sees the bill.'

'That's her problem. I give her enough to cover those things, and in any case it's her fault. She can damn' well pay for it.

'I see.'

'I'm just glad that Kate had someone to talk to.'

'Yes, I'm sorry things aren't good for you just now. It's a horrible situation to be in.'

'It's not pleasant,' he admitted. 'I can come to terms with the fact that Helen's found someone else. At least, I'm sure I will, but the thing that sticks in my throat is that she dumped it on Kate so soon. I think she might have waited a bit longer before telling her.'

She nodded her unspoken agreement and then looked at her watch and then at him, no doubt as surprised as he was that their conversation had gone the way it had. 'I really have to go, Frank,' she said, 'but honestly, if I can be of any more help you'll let me know, won't you?' She picked up her bags. 'I'm glad we've had this chat.'

'Me too. Let me carry those out for you.' He hooked his fingers through her three carrier bags and picked up his own.

'Thanks, I'm parked quite near the exit.'

They walked out to her car. She lifted the tailgate and took the bags from him. 'See you on Sunday?' She was smiling again.

'Yes. Don't worry, it'll be OK.'

Eventually Kate asked, 'What have you been working on?'

'A comedy about three blokes on a canal boat holiday in the Midlands. It's good.'

'It sounds like *Three Men in a Boat*, except that was on the Thames.'

'It's that kind of thing, plus love interest. There has to be some of that.' In the circumstances, it probably wasn't the most appropriate subject for discussion, and he fished around for another. 'I had a call from a TV researcher this afternoon,' he said, 'about the band.'

'Yeah? Are they going to put us in the programme?'

'As far as I know. Time's very short, so they're going to use some of the news item footage. It'll only be a tiny part of a one-hour programme but they're definitely interested.'

'Great.' The remark lacked conviction and she began to look distant again.

'I met Sarah in the supermarket,' he said.

She gave him a weary look. 'Oh no, not another war of words. I couldn't stand it.'

'Not at all. We had a cosy chat in the cafeteria over a cup of freshly-ground Blue Mountain.'

'Now I know you're not serious.'

'I am. The coffee was revolting but we had a useful talk all the same.'

'No falling out?'

'None whatsoever.'

She laughed without much mirth. 'I can't imagine you going in there, you're such a snob.'

'Am not.'

'Are so too, and you've got more prejudices than there are *isms*.'

'Name them all.'

'Don't be impossible.'

'Ten then.'

'All right.' She began counting on her fingers. 'Folk singers, skate boarders, people who get intellectual about pop music, people who talk in clichés...' She hung on to her third finger, searching her memory. 'Lots more. Anyway, what did you talk about?'

'Misunderstandings. We ironed a few out.'

The news was evidently a welcome surprise. 'Oh good, she's really nice when you get to know her. She's a laugh and she's dead easy to talk to.'

'Surprisingly easy.'

Her smile faded. 'I talk to her sometimes,' she said.

'I know, she told me.' There was nothing to be gained by avoiding the subject and it was looming ever nearer.

'It's so ridiculous,' she protested. 'I handled the separation and the divorce proceedings. They seemed like no big deal after all the falling out, and I think I'd got used to the idea before ever it happened.'

'I know.' In the absence of anything to say he stroked her hand.

'She told me on Sunday afternoon, and the next I knew she'd gone out with him again. That's when it hit me. It's just so *unlike* her.'

'I know.' He wasn't surprised that the poor kid had spent an age on the phone to Sarah. After a moment's thought he said, 'The excitement has to burn itself out soon. I mean, it can't go on like this for much longer.'

'You think it might be a flash in the pan?' Tears were not far away but she looked hopeful.

'To some extent, yes,' he prevaricated. He had no idea really, but if it helped her to think on those lines he wasn't going to stop her.

'I never know what's going to happen next. I wake up and suddenly there's a new development and I find I'm the only one who knew nothing about it.'

'Fair comment.' He knew he'd been as guilty as anyone of keeping things from her, to protect her, he supposed. Now he wasn't sure that it had been the best thing to do. 'I know it hasn't been easy in the past,' he said, 'but if there's anything you want to know, I mean anytime—'

She held up her hand. 'Not now, Dad. I'm so full up I couldn't take any more.'

'You're right. Let's leave it there for now and concentrate on a little diversion I have to put to you.'

'A diversion?'

'Yes, something that could make life seem less cruel.

'What is it?'

'I wondered if you'd like to do a spot of shopping on your afternoon off or whenever you and your friends can get together. I imagine clothes are high on your agenda as usual. Is there anything that particularly grabs your fancy?'

She thought for a moment. 'There is one thing I've seen. Something I'd kill for actually, but I can't really afford it.'

'That's a shame.'

She looked at him out of the corner of her eye.

'Still,' he said, 'you've got to have clothes, especially in this climate.'

'Ah well, it's rather special.' She looked apologetic. 'Now I'm working at the teashop I could chip in.'

'Quite right.'

'I mean, you give me money, which is great, but it's better if I find some of it.'

'Agreed.'

'Dan works at the swimming pool in Beckworth.'

It was interesting that she should bring Dan's name into the conversation but he didn't remark on it. Instead, he said, 'That's a good example to follow, but how much is this fabulous garment?'

In the privacy of the flat she still whispered in his ear. He gave an expression of horror. 'Thank God I don't have to pay that for my clothes. I'd never leave the house. Of course, it means we'll be living on bread and dripping for the rest of the week.'

'What's that?'

'Be thankful you don't know. Are these things very special?'

'And how!'

'I mean would they make you feel pretty good about things?'

'Oh yes.'

'In that case it's bread and dripping for dinner.' The sum involved would be a small price to pay for a diversion and a bit of happiness. His problem would wait until later when he would lose himself in the band arrangements. It was becoming a familiar refuge.

## 19

The woman who came into the ballroom with Martin looked so confident that Frank wondered if she also might be wearing concealed but expensive designer garments. Somehow he doubted it. It was more likely that she was just as good as Martin had said. He thought she might be in her fifties. She looked very neat in a flowered cotton dress and her half-framed glasses gave her the appearance of a benign headmistress. Martin introduced her to Hutch and Frank.

'This is Mrs Wainwright,' he said. He introduced the two men.

'Vanessa,' she told them with a coy smile. 'Do you want me to audition?'

'I'm sure it won't be necessary,' said Frank. 'Martin recommended you and that's good enough for us.'

'Oh good,' she said. 'Shall I go to the piano?'

'Not yet,' Hutch told her. 'Just take a seat and relax for a few minutes while I make some announcements.'

He took up his usual position in front of the band and waited for quiet.

'Good morning everybody. I've got some announcements to make before we start. First of all I'd like to welcome Vanessa Wainwright who's come to play the piano. I know you'll all make her welcome.' He stopped while the others made themselves known to her. 'Secondly, I want you to welcome Malcolm, Tricia and Heather. They've decided that the new orchestra's not for them and they want to play out with us instead.' He indicated three violinists who were standing uncertainly in one corner. 'Thirdly, I've been listening to the recording from last Saturday and I'm very impressed. Copies will be forthcoming.' He beamed at them as he delivered the last piece of news. 'Finally,' he said, 'as a result of our televised appearance we've got a gig, and it's only two weeks away.' He waited patiently again for the reaction to die down. 'It's a forties night, this time at Ferne House Country Club near Skipton and it's very posh, so you'll all have to be on your best behaviour.' He picked up an envelope and a padded bag and said, 'There's some fan mail too.' He grinned at Norman. 'One's for Mr Barraclough and the other's for Ida.' He handed them both to Norman, who slit open the envelope curiously.

'By heck, listen to this,' he said.

'"Dear Mr Barraclough,
Thank you very much for helping us with our project we enjoyed hearing about your experiences in the war it was very interesting."'

He ignored the jeers from the rest of the band and continued.

'"The band was good as well the old people enjoyed it very much the bits they liked best were the funny dances where they acted daft and the man who sang but the band was good too. We heard you were on telly. We didn't see it because we never watch the news but Jane Lawrence's mum said it was good. We hope your dog is better now.

Yours sincerely,

Matthew Briggs, Debbie Highworth and Sean Edmonds, Class 6RWE, Albion Street Middle School."'

There was a murmur of appreciation and then Norman opened the package. It contained a note and a bag of dog treats. 'What the heck! Here, listen to this.'

'I hope you're not going to read your fan mail to us every week,' said Geoff. 'We'll never get anything done.'

'You're only jealous because you haven't got any, and this is addressed to Ida anyway, so just be quiet and listen.

'"Dear Ida,

I saw you on the news and was sorry to hear that you have not been well.

I hope you make a speedy recovery and enjoy the enclosed gift.

Yours admiringly,

Scruff (dachshund cross) XXX."'

'This is what it means to be a celebrity,' said Hutch. 'I hope it won't change her.'

'It'll change her waist measurement if she goes on getting presents like this,' said Norman. He fed one of the treats to her and put the bag in his pocket. 'Scruff indeed. Next thing I know she'll be plagued with tabloid reporters and photographers with long lenses.'

'That's the price of fame,' said Hutch. 'Right, Frank, we're ready for you.' He took his place in the reed section.

'Fine. 'Morning, everyone. "You're the Cream in My Coffee". Think yourselves into it and let's hear excitement from the first note. Are you all right there, Vanessa?'

'Yes, thank you, Frank.'

'Malcolm, Tricia and Heather?'

'The three violinists nodded eagerly.

'Ready, Dan?'

'Ready, Frank.'

'OK, Let's go.' The enthusiasm was there and waiting. He could see it in their faces, including Kate's. She smiled quickly at him before tucking her violin under her chin.

The returning violinists were at the bar, happy to be accepted and catching up with their old colleagues. Vanessa sat beside Hutch.

'So what do you think, Vanessa?' he asked. 'Would you like to play out with us?'

'Oh yes, please. I had so much fun this morning and everyone's made me feel very welcome.'

'It could be a long-term job. I called in to see Eddie yesterday and he was much the same.'

'Poor old Eddie,' said Geoff, shaking his head and moving his stool to let Thomas in.

'Have you met our first trumpet, Vanessa?' asked Hutch. 'We call him "Thomas the Trumpet".'

'Actually,' said Thomas, taking Vanessa's hand, 'I was always "Davies the Lip" in Dolgellau, where I grew up. It was on account of the mushroom lip, the red pressure mark you get from the mouthpiece, see? It sort of set me apart from the other boys from an early age.'

'Oh, I love Wales,' said Vanessa. 'I've had lots of holidays there.'

'I haven't been back for ages,' Thomas admitted, 'though I've been tempted on occasions. I can't say I haven't, and it's not as if it's far, I know, but I've lost touch with all the people I knew.'

'You've eaten the lotus leaf,' said Frank. 'You're not the first to grow roots here.'

Hutch turned for the moment to Sarah, who had squeezed her stool in beside Frank. 'Hello, Sarah. What's new?' He was clearly intrigued that she had chosen not to avoid Frank as usual.

'I've been thinking of some ways of making this forties evening a bit different,' she said. 'I'll talk to you and Frank about it when I've got something more definite.'

'Good girl.'

'I need to ask Julie about what we've got in the way of gobos – lighting effects, that is. Also, I don't know what they've got at Ferne House, but we'll probably need to take our portable lights if we can.'

'If all I need is my drum kit,' said Bernard, 'there'll be room for the lights and audio stuff in my van.'

'Brilliant. Thanks, Bernard. I'll have a word with Julie now, if she hasn't left already.'

'She's over there.' Frank pointed to a table by the door, where Julie was sitting with Kate and Dan.

When Sarah had left the group, Hutch turned to Frank and asked, 'Have you two finally got the bricks down then?'

Frank nodded.

'Good lad.'

'It was her doing, not mine.'

'The main thing,' said Hutch, 'is that everybody's happy and nothing's happening to rock the boat.'

'That's right,' said Thomas. 'This is the happiest set-up I've known for a long time.'

It was noticeable that, since his short conversation with Vanessa, his accent had become more pronounced.

. . .

In the two weeks that followed Frank had little time to reflect on developments within the band. In the absence of scores and parts he was required to provide several arrangements, but those and the regular practices represented his only involvement with the band. The remainder of his time was taken up with sessions. He was called promptly by Anvil Productions to record the score for *The Droitwich Diamond* and then by Midas Studios for a recording of some songs he had arranged. After that, he was ready for the Ferne House gig.

## 20

'Four-and-twenty virgins came down from Inverness,
And when the ball was over there were four-and-twenty less …'

The boys were in a coach party mood. The budget had only run to a fifteen-seater, which meant that some of the band had to go by car, and their absence had conveniently created an all-male party.

The driver grinned at Frank. 'What are they like when they've had a few drinks?'

'Much better. They can remember more of the words then.'

As if in confirmation, the song soon dwindled to nothing and was followed by 'Sing Us Another One, Do'. The object was that each member of the party in turn had to sing a limerick. Vernon was first.

'A second trombonist from Rio,
Was seducing a lady named Cleo.
As she lowered her panties, she said, "No *andantes*,
I want it *allegro con brio*!"'

The others carolled their appreciation.

'That was a horrible song,
Sing us another one, just like the other one,
Sing us another one, do-o.'

'Bloody hell,' said the driver, 'it's like one of them regimental reunion jobs.'

'Very similar, I imagine.'

'What sort of music do you play?'

'We're a dance band. It's mainly pre-war stuff.'

The driver wrinkled his nose. 'I can't say I know any of that. I like Barry Manilow myself.' He looked wistfully at the cassette in his tape player.

'Ah well, if we all liked the same thing most of us would never get tickets, would we? And those who did would pay the earth for them.'

'That's true.'

Geoff launched into his verse.

'An Argentine gaucho called Bruno,
Told the press, "If there's one thing I do know,
A woman is fine, a boy is divine,
But a lama is *numero uno*!"'

Frank looked at the road sign ahead and covered a yawn. Thank God they were nearly there. He felt a tap on his shoulder.

'Are you all right, Frank?' asked Hutch. 'You're even quieter than usual.'

'I'm fine, thanks. Just a bit tired.'

Hutch considered that information and asked, 'Too much bed and not enough sleep?'

'I wish.' He had spent most of the night working on arrangements for the band.

'Here it is,' the driver called out. 'Ferne House Country Club.' He made a left turn into a driveway that led directly to a large, modern building. They recognised Bernard's van and two other cars in the car park.

'Sarah's party's here,' remarked Hutch, 'and I think the other car's Thomas's.'

An anxious man with a thin moustache and wearing a *Wermacht* uniform came over to introduce himself. 'I'm Brian Holdsworth,' he said, 'Club Secretary. Please don't mock. Fancy dress is mandatory tonight, and I couldn't get a British uniform.' He was clearly worried about the distinction.

Hutch offered his hand solemnly. '*Heil Hitler*. I'm Jack Hutchins and this is Frank Morrison, our bandleader.'

'You just had to say something like that, didn't you? I knew somebody would before ever I put this lot on.' Brian looked hurt rather than annoyed. 'I usually stay aloof from this sort of thing, you know. I like to preserve my dignity, but the committee decided in its wisdom that absolutely everybody had to dress up. I don't mind telling you, I shan't be able to show my face after this.'

Frank felt sorry for him. 'You'll be all right when the others arrive,' he said, 'when everyone's in fancy dress.' He felt like a parent at the school gates.

'But what's the betting I'm the only German here?'

'You'll probably win a prize,' said Hutch.

Brian gave a final look of despair. 'Oh, to hell with it,' he said, 'you'd better come inside. Some of your people are already here.' He led the way to the function room, where Julie and Sarah were rigging the lights. Brian excused himself to check the tables.

'I see you've met the shrinking storm-trooper,' said Sarah. 'Poor Brian. It's going to be a big party and the members are bringing lots of guests.' She looked round to check that Brian was properly out of earshot and said, 'Some of them are members of one of those clubs that go everywhere in military vehicles and they all dress up in American uniforms. Brian's expecting the car park to be filled with tanks and lorries.'

'It's just as well we brought the big band stuff then. We'll mix it in with our usual numbers.'

'Right on, Hutch. These people have jive and jitterbug nights. They're terribly keen.'

Hutch looked at her slyly and said, 'You'll be all right. You can do that gyrating stuff, can't you?'

'Not dressed like this.' She pointed to her black trousers and top. 'I'm strictly backstage.'

'Well, I think you ought to put something glamorous on and give us a turn on the dance floor.'

She looked over her shoulder at him matter-of-factly and said, 'Forget it.' She gave a wing nut a few more turns and then spoke again, as if as an afterthought. 'Frank, can we have a word about an idea I've had? Not now, but before we get under way?'

'Sure, any time.'

'See if you can talk her into dancing for us while you're at it,' Hutch told him.

'Beat it, buster.' She waved a valedictory hand. 'We're busy here and you're holding the job up. The band room's to the left of where Bernard's put his drums. See you later, Frank.'

They walked over to the band area.

'I can't get over the way she calls you "Hutch",' said Frank. 'It seems odd somehow.'

'She's called me that for years, and anyway, she knows I never liked her calling me "Granddad". It made me feel like an old man.'

'Heaven forbid.' Frank dismissed the thought and stepped into the band room.

'Have you seen what's arriving?' Thomas gestured through the window. 'They could wage a sizeable war with what they've got out there.'

Some of them went to look and Geoff said, 'They pay a fortune for them things, you know.'

Dennis Birch wasn't impressed. 'Well, they're Yanks, aren't they?'

'They're not Yanks, you dipstick. They're only dressed up to look like Yanks. These characters are from Lancashire. I've been talking to one of them.'

'What for?'

''Cause I'm not a miserable sod like you.'

'Ready, everybody,' called Frank. He held the door while they filed into the band area. After the obligatory wait until the shuffling had stopped he walked on and started 'The Sun Has Got His Hat On'.

The applause was generous. Most of the members and their guests were in uniform of one kind or another. There were land girls, sailors, airmen, ATS girls, soldiers and some ingeniously clad civilians. One woman wearing an open trench coat over a scanty outfit looked remarkably like Marlene Dietrich, and another had found an SS tunic, which she wore with a tiny black miniskirt and thigh boots. Brian was not the only German after all.

The mix of music seemed to be working well too. The occasional big band numbers; 'Green Eyes', 'In the Mood' and 'Moonlight Serenade' were popular, and judging by the smiles and nods from passing dancers the band's usual repertoire was going down well. Frank could see that the musicians were happy. Their faces told him that in their different ways. Geoff was beaming as usual, Bernard raised one eloquent eyebrow as he went into a particularly impressive piece of stick work, and from the piano, Vanessa's eyes twinkled behind her half-frame glasses.

It was after Dan had gone off to energetic applause that one of the guests in US Army uniform tapped Frank on the shoulder.

'Say, buddy,' he said, 'can't you play something a little hotter? We wanna cut loose, you know?'

The request sounded odd in a Lancashire accent, and Frank hesitated for a moment but he managed to respond appropriately. 'Wait 'til the second half,' he said. 'That's when you and your buddies'll get a piece of the action.'

The GI looked reassured.

Two waitresses arrived in the band room at the break, carrying trays of drinks and Brian followed them. 'It's going well,' he said breathlessly, 'much better than I expected. The members are having a good time but I must say I'm a bit uneasy about some of the guests. I won't have anything improper.'

'Calm down,' Hutch told him. 'Everything's under control.'

'Oh, it had better be, because if there's anything untoward I'll stamp on it.' He gestured with one jackboot to show that he meant it.

'That's the spirit, Brian.' Hutch fastened his top button for him and patted his shoulder.

'Right then, I'll be around if you need me.'

'Don't worry. We'll shout.'

Geoff returned to the band room looking impressed. 'I think it's amazing, the lengths these people go to for authenticity,' he said. 'I've just been talking to one of them. You know, he's got the booklet they gave all the Americans, the one that told them how to behave when they came to Britain.'

'Useful when you come from Manchester,' said Hutch.

'And he's even got a packet of chewing gum and a pair of nineteen-forties nylon stockings in his pocket.'

Kate frowned. 'What's he got them for?'

Sarah enlightened her.

Frank asked, 'Are you all set up, Sarah?'

'Yes, Julie's rigged up the spare mike.' She nodded to where Dan was leafing through his music, nervously going over his words. 'He's not the only one who's nervous.'

'Don't worry, it'll be fine.'

Soon it was time to start the second half. The band began with 'Limehouse Blues' and followed it with Dan's favourite solo, 'A Nightingale Sang in Berkeley Square'. Julie brought down the lights on the band and switched to a soft violet filter, leaving only Dan under the white spotlight. He sang the song with such conviction that his audience was reluctant to let him go, but it was time for something different. The next number was for the man and his friends who wanted to cut loose. The lights came up and the band went into 'Sliphorn Jive'. The style was a complete departure for them but they were playing well and their self-confidence was burgeoning.

Frank turned to watch the dancing couples, some of whom had opted for the Lindy Hop. It was a popular dance and more of them began to join in. Some of them were hopeless, others were quite good, and a few were truly excellent. One pair in particular caught his eye. They were putting everything into their routine. He swung her to his right and left, and then she zoomed between his legs and reappeared, surprisingly upright behind him. After that their moves became increasingly extravagant. Other couples were performing aerials, but this girl was flying higher than the rest, clearing her partner's shoulders by inches and descending athletically behind him. They seemed to be going for a record, because with each throw she appeared to gain altitude, and each time she gave way to gravity her full skirt billowed like a parachute, favouring onlookers with a glimpse of nineteen-forties underwear. Frank saw what Geoff meant about authenticity.

The floor was soon cleared for the skyrocketing couple. Everyone else had taken to the tables to watch the performance, and from the band room door, the driver of the minibus looked on in fascination. The only one who wasn't impressed was Brian, who stood poised and outraged on the edge of the floor. It was inevitable that as guardian of the Club's good name he should intervene.

There was a moan of disappointment from the onlookers when he strode across the floor, but it must have been inaudible to the jiving couple because they seemed unaware of his presence as they continued to leap in every direction. Such was the variety of their repertoire that Brian was repeatedly frustrated in his attempts to make contact with either of them. As soon as he was in a position to speak to one, he or she was whisked away from him. Frank reckoned that they must be aware of his presence by now and that they thought he was either a harmless drunk or someone to be ignored anyway. Moreover, the volume of the music must have made it impossible for them to hear what he was saying and he went unheeded in the excitement. The drama hadn't passed unnoticed by the band. Some were craning forward to get a better view, and Geoff and Norman, who were tacet for four bars, were ducking and weaving like spectators at a boxing match, lending distant encouragement to the frustrated secretary.

Amid jeers from the members and guests, Brian struggled to attract the couple's attention, and the band was winding up to the big finish when he eventually managed to touch the man's shoulder. By that time it was too late for the couple to stop. They were already in mid launch; the girl was hurtling skyward and the unfortunate Brian failed to move quickly enough. With the accuracy of a circus acrobat she landed squarely in front of him and brought them both down in a crumpled heap.

The soldier turned angrily, and then seeing his partner on the floor, knelt urgently beside her. With only his lower half visible, Brian was forgotten for the moment.

The band managed to see out the number before giving in to mirth, but their laughter turned rapidly into concern. Some of the members approached the huddle on the floor, alerted by the lack of movement.

The GI helped his partner carefully into a sitting position. Still dazed, she sat motionless for a while and then with a look of absent curiosity, lifted the hem of her skirt to reveal Brian, who emerged slowly from between her knees, blinking like a startled tortoise. Gingerly, they allowed themselves to be helped from the floor to a spontaneous round of applause.

Frank walked to the mike and the babble of chatter stopped. A man in a spiv suit was trying to attract his attention. He pointed to Brian and the girl and gave Frank the thumbs up sign.

'It's good news,' Frank announced into the microphone. 'It looks as if they're both going to be OK.' He waited for the cheer from around the room to die down, and continued. 'Let's have a gentle number now.' There was a burst of ironic laughter. 'Let's dance, or just listen if you wish, to "Blue Moon".' The lights over the band changed to dark blue, and a shifting nightscape with twinkling stars appeared, projected on to the back wall.

Frank began to relax. If they were never asked to Ferne House again, at least he was going to enjoy the rest of the programme. He led the band into the first chorus, and he knew they were enjoying it too because they were playing their own kind of music again. Hutch was playing with deep commitment, no doubt thinking the same thing and unaware of what was about to happen. As they went into a short bridge passage Frank looked to the band room door, where

Sarah was standing by a microphone. He gave her a beat's warning and then cued her in.

Hutch looked up, startled for the moment. Then he beamed and winked at Frank.

Frank was impressed too. Her voice had a warm, smooth quality, and there was also something of Dan's ability to communicate the lyrics. Their styles were different, but Frank reckoned that they would sound pretty good together if he could arrange it.

At the end, the dancers applauded loudly. They must have wondered who and where the singer was, but they would have to wait, because the next dance was a quickstep and they were going to play 'All I do is Dream of You' without a vocal.

There were two more invisible performances by Sarah and a solo by Dan before Frank turned to the dancers to thank them and to round off the evening.

'Before we play our last number,' he said, 'I'd like you to meet some people who don't usually find their way into the limelight, but without whom none of this would make sense. First of all, give a big hand, please, for the technical wonder behind our sound, lighting and special effects: Julie Wilson! Come on, Julie.' He took her hand and pulled her into her own spotlight. 'Take a bow. Good girl.' He kissed her on the cheek and let her resume her position, embarrassed but appreciated, at the lighting console. 'Finally, another big hand, please, for our Artistic Director and mystery female vocalist, Sarah Hutchins!'

Sarah threaded her way through the band, frowning at him in mock anger. She took her bow and inclined her cheek. 'You bastard, Frank,' she murmured. 'I'll kill you for this.'

'It's become a tradition with the band to play the same closing number,' he told the partygoers. 'It's "Good Night, Sweetheart", and here again to sing it is the Man with the Velvet Voice, Dan Bairstow!'

'I thought it was great.' Andy the driver was a convert. 'It wasn't just the bird flashing her undies – I liked the music as well. Where are you playing next?'

'Give us your phone number,' Hutch told him, 'and we'll keep you posted.' He sat beside Frank and the minibus moved off. 'Well done, Frank,' he said. 'Hey, that was a turn up, wasn't it, young Sarah singing for us? I told you she had a grand voice.'

'She has, Hutch,' he agreed wearily, 'but what I can't understand is how someone who teaches performance arts can be so shy about taking a curtain call.'

'It's because you brought her on stage without her make up and finery on, you daft article. You know what women are like.'

'I suppose so.' He'd never associated those things with Sarah, but Hutch knew her better than he did. It was too much for his brain to wrestle with. He was aware that Hutch was saying something else to him but he couldn't make sense of it. He felt his eyes closing and knew he was falling asleep.

## 21

On Monday came the sad news that Eddie had suffered a second, fatal stroke. It had happened on Friday, but the first anyone in the band heard of it was from Hutch, who had called at the hospital on Monday morning. The funeral had been arranged for the following Thursday, and Frank was noting it in his diary when the phone rang again.

'Frank, it's Pat-sy.'

'Hi, Patsy.' He tried out the notes on the piano and found that they weren't E,E,A,G as he'd thought, but a semitone lower, which made them two E flats, an A flat and a G flat.

'Have I caught you at a busy time?' Patsy's voice interrupted his musings. 'I can hear the piano.'

'No, just trying something out.'

'Good. I may have something for you soon but the music's still under discussion so I can't tell you anything more definite.'

'I'll be patient.'

'You're too patient, Frank. You should try being more assertive occasionally.'

'Could you imagine that?'

'Maybe not. Better just stay as you are for now. Oh, and thanks for the tape of the band.' I'm terribly impressed. So is everyone else who's heard it.'

'That's the spirit, Patsy. Spread the word.'

'Oh, but I do. Anyway, how is the band?'

'Ah well, I heard this morning that our pianist has died.'

'Oh, no.'

'He'd been ill, and we'd already got someone to stand in for him but it's a tragedy all the same. He was a nice bloke.'

'What's the stand-in like?'

'Good. She looks like someone's maiden aunt, a middle-aged Mary Poppins, but she's an excellent pianist.'

'So you can carry on. That's good. You know the documentary is scheduled for the new year, don't you?'

'Yes, I had a call from them a short time ago.'

'They squeezed you in at the last minute. They were already at the editing stage but they thought the story was worth using.'

'It was really good of you to fix it up.'

'Well, you know, I cast my bread on the waters. Anyway, I'll be in touch.' It was good that things were moving again.

He looked at the CDs on his desk. In the absence of scores, there were two numbers to be arranged; 'Smoke Gets in Your Eyes' and 'Embraceable You'. The first was a dance number that called for a female vocalist, and the delicate orchestration that it demanded was now made possible by the presence of the new string players. The other was to be strictly a band item.

Through the window he could see a figure approaching the flats from the direction of Providence Mills. It was the Candidate for the Promotion of Regional Produce on her daily training stint. She must be phenomenally fit with all that exercise. He watched her pass under his window and then disappear towards the railway bridge. The rear view was quite delightful.

He decided to practise being more assertive by making himself concentrate on the arrangements.

...

It was a week of telephone interruptions of which Helen's was the least welcome. She phoned him on Thursday as he was changing to go to the funeral. It was the first time they'd spoken since Kate had moved back in with her.

'How are you keeping?' There was little warmth in her enquiry.

'Well, thanks, and you?'

'I'm OK. Well, actually, I'm not.'

'Oh?'

'It's nothing terrible, just the usual.'

'Bad luck.' Heavy and prolonged periods would be a handicap in her new lifestyle.

'The thing is, I have to go into hospital, just briefly.'

'For a hysterectomy?'

'No, nothing as drastic as that. Just a D and C, but I don't want to wait forever. I thought I'd have it done privately.'

'OK, I'll send you a claim form.'

'Thanks. You know how I feel about queue-jumping but this has gone on too long.'

'Quite.' He remembered the argument they'd had when he took out the policy. 'I'm sure you'll square it with your conscience.'

'Don't be cheap, Frank. The policy's there so I may as well use it.'

'While you can,' he agreed, 'because you won't be on it for much longer. Anyway, to change the subject quickly because I'm changing to go out, how's Kate?'

'Impossible.'

'By that, do you mean insecure, hurt, angry, resentful?'

'If you must sound like a thesaurus, yes. She's also disenchanted with her job at the café. I knew it wouldn't last long, she's been so used to getting money the easy way, from you.'

He looked at his watch. He had to be off soon. 'What's been happening?'

'She won't tell me anything. You know what she's like.'

'I'll speak to her about it.'

'Yes, you'll be seeing her this afternoon, won't you? I assume you're both going to the same funeral.'

'We are, as it happens.' No wonder Kate wouldn't talk to her if that was the extent of her interest in her daughter's life.

'One more thing, Frank. The grass needs cutting. Robert offered to do it for me, but he can't start the mower.'

'I've never had a problem with it.'

'It's ready for the scrap heap.'

Suddenly he bridled. 'Who says?'

'Robert.'

'That's hardly an expert opinion, and anyway, he can keep his grubby hands off my mower.'

'But the lawns are getting out of hand.'

'So pay someone else to do it. I give you enough money.'

There was a few seconds' gratifying silence and then she said, 'Frank, what's got into you?'

'I'll tell you what's got into me. A ham-fisted, mechanically-inept tax gatherer is buggering up my daughter's life and, incredibly, her mother is encouraging him to do it. Now, I've got a funeral to go to. I'll send you the forms. Goodbye.' He replaced the phone and looked up at his confidant. 'That told her, Wyatt,' he said. 'I think I'm getting the hang of this assertiveness thing.' The peace officer gazed back, mildly impressed.

He had to crawl behind the cortège all the way to the crematorium but at least he wouldn't be late for the funeral. It was twenty-past two and the funeral was at two-thirty, so he reckoned he must be following the right hearse.

All the way he was bugged by Helen's phone call. The bloody cheek of it, muscling in on the domestic scene and, on top of that, criticising his faithful old Suffolk Colt. It was enough to try any reasonable man's patience. It hadn't taken the Sheriff of Nottingham long to persuade Helen to have something done about her problem either. Next, she'd be able to go back on the pill and they'd both be sitting pretty. Well, not sitting exactly. If the man in her life lacked the ingenuity to start a lawn mower he was unlikely to be inventive in the bedroom.

Once, for the novelty, Frank remembered, Helen and he had done it on the stairs. It was only once, because his toes had lost their grip on the stair carpet and he'd bounced on every step on his way down, like a rag doll on a pogo stick. He still winced and crossed his legs at the recollection.

The hearse eventually turned left into the crematorium driveway and the cortège caterpillared after it. Frank could see Hutch and Kate among the small gathering in the car park. Kate spotted the car and joined him.

'I didn't know what to wear,' she told him through the car window. She looked down at her black orchestra dress. 'Some people don't seem to have bothered much.'

It was true. There were friends or family – Frank wasn't sure which – who were dressed quite casually, as if they were going out for a drink. 'You did right,' he told her. 'Some of us have to set an example.' He felt more protective of her than usual because it was her first funeral. 'Let's go inside,' he said, giving her his arm so that they could join the end of the procession entering the chapel.

After a welcome and a reading by the minister, Eddie's eldest son mumbled a eulogy. It would have been better left to the minister, but it seemed to Frank that it was up to people to do things their own way. Even so, the bare string of facts said little of Eddie as a person, which was sad. Frank lost interest and began to look around the chapel. He identified Hutch, Vernon, Geoff, Dan and a few others from behind. Sarah evidently hadn't made it. Norman was there, and he imagined Ida must be in the car. A notice outside barred all except guide dogs. As Helen was frequently inclined to remark, inequality was still a fact of life.

Eddie's son sat down and the minister called on Hutch to speak. Frank paid attention again and listened to a proper account of the man he'd known.

Hutch spoke about Eddie's heartbreak at Dorothy's death, and his retreat into seclusion. He told of how he had consented to join the band and how it had given him another reason for living. It was sad, he said, that Eddie's time with the NADO had been so brief, but the stroke had occurred when he'd just taken part in a practice and when he was enjoying a drink with his fellow musicians. He had died a happy man.

Tears were pooling in Kate's eyes. Frank squeezed her hand and found her a tissue.

After final prayers, everyone filed out. They shook hands with the minister and Eddie's sons and daughter, who invited them back to the Craven Heifer.

'Do we have to go, Dad?' Kate waited to ask him until they were in the car park.

'We don't have to, but I'm always worried that no one will turn up, and I'd hate to be part of that.' He could see that she was uneasy and he didn't want to leave her to go home alone. 'I'll tell you what,' he said, 'let's see if Hutch and the others are going.'

'We're going all right.' Norman appeared beside them. 'We've got to see Eddie off properly. Don't worry, flower,' he told Kate, 'you'll be all right with us.' He touched Frank's arm and pointed to Thomas and Vanessa, who were leaving the group. 'I think young Thomas and the merry widow have taken a shine to each other.'

'Young Thomas is about ten years older than me,' said Frank.

'Aye well, it's on occasions like this that I feel the difference. Anyroad, I'd best find little Vernon. I'm giving him a lift.'

'Isn't Hutch going?'

'Aye, he'll be going with Sarah.'

Frank scanned the car park and eventually spotted Hutch. He was standing with a woman in sunglasses. She bore little resemblance to Sarah.

He let Kate into the car. 'It's a miracle I got here on time,' he told her. 'Your mum phoned just as I was ready to leave.'

'What did she want?'

'Just the health insurance things. You know she's going to have some treatment, don't you?' They joined the queue for the main road.

'Oh, that.' She sounded unimpressed. 'To be honest, I'm sick of hearing about it. She spent half an hour on the phone describing her yucky symptoms to Lynne from her *T'ai chi* class.'

'Never mind. She said you were unhappy at the teashop. What's been happening there?'

'Oh, nothing much.'

'Come on, Kate, something's obviously not right.' He parked on the road outside the Craven Heifer.

Her lips tightened. 'It's nothing really.'

'In that case you can tell me about it. I mean it's not as if we're strangers.'

'Oh, Dad…'

'Sorry, but I'm concerned and I'm going nowhere until you've told me.'

'Oh, hell.' She stared out of the window. 'It's just that… it's not the job, it's the customers.'

'Go on.' The others were arriving at the pub but this was important.

'Not all the customers, just two of them, two men that come in for lunch every day. They… well, they're too friendly.' She was still looking through the window.

'Go on.' He was angry already.

'Well, it wasn't too bad at first. They just kept saying things, trying to embarrass us, but now they can't keep their hands to themselves. They're absolutely foul.'

He had half expected something of the kind but he was still stunned. He managed to say, 'I wish you'd told me about this before.'

'We thought they'd get bored with it and stop doing it.'

'What's the manageress done about it?'

'She doesn't know. She hasn't been well, and there's only us there and Denise in the kitchen, and she just tells us to ignore them. She's not very bright.' She looked at him, appealing. 'I don't want a fuss, Dad. I'd rather leave the job.'

'What time do they come in?'

'Dad, please, I really don't want a fuss.'

'There won't be one. When do they come in?'

'About one o'clock, a little bit after one, but Dad—'

'There'll be nothing to be embarrassed about, believe me.'

'I wish I hadn't told you now.' She looked down into her lap.

'And I'm glad you did. Come on, let's go inside.' They left the car and went in to join the others.

He took Kate for another quick word with the family and then stood aside for someone else.

Hutch was standing by the bar and it seemed natural for them to join him.

'Hi, Hutch.'

'Hello, you two.' They shook hands formally, as friends do at funerals.

'Hello, Frank and Kate.' Sarah offered her cheek to Frank and then hugged Kate. 'It's not very nice, is it? Bear up, it'll soon be over.'

Frank suddenly found himself at a complete disadvantage. He'd barely recognised her at first, but to tell her that would be crass. It would also be a criticism of the way she usually looked. Instead, he asked lamely, 'Can I get you people a drink?'

'The first one's on Eddie.' Hutch indicated a row of glasses filled with wine. Another row contained fruit juice. He picked up two glasses of red wine and handed one to Kate, saying, 'This'll make you feel better.'

'Dan's over by the door,' Sarah told her. 'He's been looking out for you.' Kate looked to where she was pointing, saw Dan and filtered through the crowd to join him.

Hutch asked, 'Is this her first one?'

'Yes, they've never figured in her life before now. She was even worried about what to wear, and her mother wasn't sufficiently interested to offer advice.' He knew that there must have been times when he'd fallen short, when possibly work had come between Kate and him, but it didn't make him less angry.

'I think she got it about right,' said Sarah.

He took in Sarah's hair, now down to her shoulders. With that, a little make up and a simple black dress she had effected a transformation.

She had evidently read his mind. 'You didn't think I'd come to a funeral in backstage gear, did you?'

'Of course not.' He smiled awkwardly. 'Although to be honest, I was hoping you'd leave your hair band at home.'

'I'm going to circulate,' said Hutch. 'I'll leave you to dig yourself out of this one, Frank.' He touched Sarah's arm and said, 'Don't make him do it all by himself.' He sidled away to talk to someone else.

'I'm sorry,' said Frank, 'I'm saying all the wrong things today.'

'I can't blame you. You've only ever seen me dressed for work, and I agree, the hair bands are a bit frumpish but they do keep it out of the way of ropes and scaffolding.'

'I'm sorry.'

'Relax. As a matter of fact, I wanted to have a word. Not here – we don't want to form a clique – but maybe we could meet sometime soon.'

'Of course.'

'It's an idea I've had. That's all.'

'Fine. Could you be in Cullington tomorrow lunchtime?'

'I could, yes.'

'I have to go to The Copper Kettle in Northgate. It's where Kate works.'

She nodded. 'I know. What's happening there?'

'A couple of creeps have been making a nuisance of themselves with the kids and I'm going to put a stop to it. I'll be suitably restrained, I promise. You can go and powder your nose while I speak to them if you like.'

'Now you know that I occasionally powder it?' She laughed.

'Oh, God.'

'It's all right. What time?'

'I'll be in there from about one.'

'Fine. What time are you expecting their company?'

'About then.'

'OK, I'll make it a bit later. It'll save powdering my nose.'

'Great.' Suddenly he felt easier. 'Kate's worried that I'll embarrass her but I wouldn't dream of it.'

'I know, but should I bring a first aid kit in case diplomacy fails?'

'No, there'll be no thick ear stuff, just sweet reason. I'm a gentle soul.'

'Of course.' She looked over his shoulder. 'Kate's coming now. We can reassure her.'

Now visibly more relaxed, Kate joined them with Dan. 'I hope you two aren't fighting,' she said.

'Not at all,' Sarah told her. 'As a matter of fact, we're going to have a business meeting over lunch tomorrow in The Copper Kettle, so don't worry. I'll make sure your dad doesn't embarrass you.'

Whatever Kate thought, she made no reply because like everyone else, she was distracted by a loud lapping noise from beneath a nearby table. Ida was giving Eddie a proper send-off.

On the way home, Kate confided that at long last she and Dan were an item. She'd waited so long for him to make a move that she'd finally taken the initiative and asked him out.

Frank wondered how long his daughter had been a brazen hussy.

## 22

Kate came to his table immediately. 'Dad,' she said, 'I really don't want you to do this.'

'Don't worry, it'll be all right. Just get me a pot of coffee while I wait for Sarah, will you?'

'OK.' She headed grimly for the kitchen.

He felt sorry for her, not knowing what to expect but still to be at the centre of so much unpleasantness. But it would soon be over. He switched his attention to the other girl, who seemed pleasant, now that he had time to notice more about her. She was dark-haired and a little taller than Kate, but about the same age. Kate said something to her and she looked across at him briefly. They must both be feeling apprehensive.

It was two minutes to one by his watch, and so far the only other customers were an elderly couple who seemed to be having trouble making their choice from the menu. Kate said something to them and they shook their heads. A minute later she brought Frank a tray with a cup and saucer and a small cafetiére.

He squeezed her hand. 'Thanks, darling. Now carry on and don't worry.'

She left him, still tight-lipped.

He had not long to wait. At about five past one, two men entered the shop and took a table not far from his. One was young, maybe in his twenties, with a brief case that must be too important to be left in the office, or maybe that was what he liked people to think. The other was just seedy, his suit was crumpled and the tips of his collar curled upwards like the corners of a well-thumbed book. He hoped these were the two. They looked like the kind of hateful bastards he was expecting.

A glimpse at Kate's face confirmed that they were. She tried not to look at him as she and her colleague approached their table. He imagined that neither was prepared to leave her friend to fend for herself. It was touching in a tragic kind of way.

He watched them carefully. The men were ordering and the girls were keeping their distance, but it did not deter the seedy one. Frank saw him wink at his friend and then reach out deliberately to slide his podgy hand under the dark-haired girl's skirt. She backed away quickly and he withdrew his hand, but that was enough for Frank. He got up and walked over to their table. The girls retreated hurriedly.

There was confusion in the men's eyes. They glanced at each other and then back to him. He leaned forward with his hands on the tabletop.

'The fair-haired one,' he told them, scarcely controlling his anger, 'is my daughter.' He was rewarded by their reaction. Shock, guilt and fear paraded across their features in gratifying succession. 'The other one isn't,' he went on, 'but as far as I know, her father can't be here today, so you'll have to take it from me instead, that if either of you touches those girls again, I promise you, you'll be taking your next meal through a drip. Do you hear me?'

'Do yourselves a favour and go now,' advised a woman's voice from behind him. 'I've seen what Al can do when he's angry.'

They stood up, scraping their chairs against the floor, and left without speaking.

The elderly man detached himself from his wife and came across the room. Curiously, he offered Frank his hand. 'May I call you Al?'

'Feel free.' Frank took his hand and felt the anger draining away.

'It was disgusting what that man did, Al. I'm glad you were here. I've spoken to them before but they just laugh at an old man like me.'

'At least you made the effort, and I'm grateful for that.' He smiled at the old man. 'Enjoy your meal.'

He took Sarah to their table and asked her, 'What's with the "Al" stuff?'

'Oh, that's just the thespian in me. I've always wanted to be in a gangster scene.'

'Al Capone was one of the bad guys.'

'I know, but "Eliot" would have sounded silly.'

'Fair enough. So what's it to be, coffee?'

'Coffee will do just fine.'

Kate came to the table.

'It's OK,' Frank told her, squeezing her hand. 'They won't bother you again.'

'Thanks, Dad.' She was blushing with relief.

'No trouble. We'd like some coffee though. A pot for two, please.'

She departed with their order, still flushed.

'I'm not really what you told them,' he said, 'but if they'd touched Kate it would have been different.'

'I know,' she touched his hand lightly. 'For a gentle soul you sure had a roscoe pointed at those schmucks' heads, but calm down. It's all done now.'

He felt himself relax. 'I liked your supporting role,' he said.

She wrinkled her nose. 'It's the story of my life. I never get to star in anything.'

'But you could so easily, especially without your hair band.'

'I'm wearing legs again too.' She swivelled in her chair to show him that she was wearing a skirt.

'Dancer's legs.' He nodded with approval.

'You betcha ass.'

'Lauren Bacall?'

'Yup, she said it first. If she hadn't, I would have.'

'What do you want to talk to me about?'

'First things first.' She scanned the menu. 'The prawn salad sounds about right.'

'Consider it yours. I'm paying.'

'Good man. It's boring, I know, but it's about Dan. I know I sound like a mother hen, but damn it, that's how it is.'

'You're talking about my daughter's new boyfriend.'

'Yes, isn't it sweet?'

'I don't know. I'm just getting used to the idea of a girl asking a boy out. They didn't do it in my day.'

'Right, but before you think about that let me make my plea on Dan's behalf.'

'Go ahead. I'm listening.'

'He did a dance number for an assessment at the end of term and he was hopeless. It was so bad his partner had to do it again with someone else to be sure of getting her grade.'

'He must feel pretty bad about that.'

'And how. His confidence is low at the best of times, and it's a vicious spiral.' She stopped when Kate brought the coffee.

'Are you ready to order?' Kate produced a pen and pad from her apron pocket.

'Sure,' said Frank. 'The broad will have da prawn salad and I'll have da ploughman's.'

'What?'

'I think the boss has bitten his tongue,' said Sarah.

'You're both mad,' said Kate. She wrote the order on her pad and left them.

'You're not only mad,' Frank observed, 'you're completely different.'

'Nope, it's all me. I just know you better now.'

'So you're convinced I'm not the poser you thought I was?'

'More or less. May I continue?'

'Do.'

She ran her finger in a circle on the table thoughtfully. 'To cut a long story short, Dan can dance with me leading him, but I've got to be careful. I could lay myself open to all kinds of accusations. On the other hand, though, if he happened to be dancing with me in another context and a video were made of it, he could submit that and there wouldn't be a problem.'

'I get your drift, but won't he have to dance on his own two feet, as it were, at some time?'

'To some extent, but dance is going to be a small part of his future. I just want him to pass at the end of the course.'

It made sense. 'Right, where do I come in?'

She lifted her elbows and leant forward. It looked as if it was going to be a big favour. 'I'd like to do a speciality number with him at one of the Exchange Club dances, just one in place of a band item. Would that be all right?'

'I don't see why not.'

'Great.' She gave him a beaming smile. 'Thanks for that.'

'What music do you have in mind?'

'Am I right in thinking that you're working on "Embraceable You" as a band number?'

'As we speak. Well, almost.'

'That would be perfect.'

'Consider it done. There's just one question.'

'Ask it.'

'What will you wear?'

She gave him a patient look. 'Don't worry, I shan't wear jeans and a T-shirt, if that's what you're afraid of.'

'Oh, good.'

'And I'll be leaving my hair band at home.'

'Phew.'

Kate put their plates on the table and looked at them suspiciously. 'Mayonnaise?' she asked. 'Thousand Island dressing? The name of a good psychiatrist?'

'Just mayonnaise for me, please,' said Sarah.

'And me.'

'Thank goodness for that.' She brought a dish of mayonnaise from the side table and set it down. 'Enjoy your meal.'

'You mentioned something about Dan's background when we spoke before,' said Frank. 'What was the problem?'

'The same as mine, except that it was his mother who did a runner when he was little. I gather his father had a tough time coping with it, and on top of that the poor chap was out of work for much of Dan's childhood.'

'Poor lad. How old were you when your father left?'

'Ten.' She tore a bread roll in half in what might have been a symbolic gesture. 'He went to live with his girlfriend. It didn't last, but he didn't come back either. I lived with Hutch and my gran until the fuss had died down. You know that my father was adopted, don't you?'

The question took Frank momentarily by surprise. 'Yes,' he said, 'they told me about it some time ago. It was during the war, I believe. Weren't his parents killed in the bombing?'

'His mother was. His father was killed at sea.' She smiled faintly. 'My real grandparents. I know nothing at all about them.'

'Do you really need to know about them?'

She shook her head decisively.

'Your adoptive grandparents were a class act on their own. Hutch still is.'

'That's very true.'

'They brought you to a concert at the Exchange, I remember. You must have been about ten.'

She nodded. 'I remember it. You seemed terribly grown up.'

'I was eighteen.'

'Yes, you don't seem quite so grown up now.'

'I'm working on it.'

'Good man.' She returned to her story. 'Anyway, I was feeling wretched and suddenly you came to find me. You gave me an Orangillo with two straws and I burst into tears.'

'Don't you like Orangillo?'

She sighed with exasperation.

'Sorry, it's a bad habit. I do it when the conversation gets intense. It must be very irritating.'

'Don't worry. I cried because I was so miserable and because your little act of kindness was more than I could take.'

'I'm sorry.'

'Don't be silly. Anyway, as I've just bared my soul to you, tell me about your father. You said he died when you were young.'

'I was three. I only know what I've been told. He was a sales rep, so he was away from home a lot.'

'What happened to him?'

'A road accident. He'd been to a conference in London and he was on his way home the same night. No one knows what happened exactly, except that his car hit a road sign on the A1 and he was found dead at the wheel. The worst thing was that my mother was left with nothing more than what was in the current account. Still,' he shrugged, 'we've all got our problems.'

A woman had left the kitchen and was approaching the table.

'Mr Morrison? I'm sorry I haven't been able to speak to you before. I've only just come back after an operation and the girls have told me what's been going on. I just wanted to thank you. I only wish I'd known about those two before.'

'I think I may have lost you two regular customers.'

'Oh, I can do without their kind. Now, will you let me tear up your bill?'

It had been a useful day.

The Showdown at The Copper Kettle had to rank highly as an instance of assertive behaviour, but before Frank could share it with Wyatt Earp the phone rang. It was Patsy and she was unusually excited.

'Frank,' she said, 'about the series I mentioned. The production team and the director have seen a video of the Northern Focus item and listened to the tape. We've made a decision about the sound track. If your boys are still in need of a boost, this should do it.'

## 23

It was more than frustrating that Frank could say nothing to the band about Patsy's decision until he'd been to a planning meeting and the details had been finalised. In the meantime, he had to keep the matter to himself throughout a practice and a meeting of the union branch, at which several members of the new orchestra congratulated band members on their TV appearance.

On his return from London however, he was able to call a special meeting for Thursday evening. Only Hutch and he knew the reason for it.

Hutch looked around at the group seated in the band room. He checked that everyone was present and began.

'We've got another gig on the twenty-second of September,' he said. 'It's a golden wedding celebration at Bentley Hall, Wakefield. We got it as a result of our TV debut and we need to sort out some more numbers fairly smartly. These people are Gershwin fans.'

'Do they do that sort of thing at Bentley Hall?' asked Dennis. 'I thought it was a private house.'

'Not now. It's a function venue. It's still very posh though, so it's best behaviour again.'

'I've heard it's very good,' said Geoff. 'They use it for wedding receptions. There's even a bridal suite. They can do everything under the same roof—'

'Ladies present, Geoff.'

'I only meant—'

'We know what you meant.' Hutch signalled him to be quiet. 'That's all I have to tell you. I'll let Frank give you his news as that's the real reason for this meeting.' There was a rare moment of silence as he took his seat. Everyone's attention was on Frank.

'After a branch meeting that none of us will ever forget,' he began, 'some of you said you wanted the band to do something big enough to make a few people sit up and take notice.' He allowed a mutter of agreement and went on. 'Well, we're going to do something special at last, and here it is. A production company I know is making a TV drama set in the Depression years, and from what I've seen of the screenplay it's going to be good.' It occurred to him that he hadn't known them so quiet since the day they learned about their exclusion from the new orchestra.

'The music is going to consist of existing songs,' he continued, 'and to accommodate special lyrics there'll be three new songs that I'm going to write in the period style. Now, here's the punch line – the NADO is being asked to record the complete track. We'll do it in four three-hour sessions and the producer wants to fit the first two sessions in before Christmas.'

There was a collective indrawn breath, but he went on. 'This isn't something I've wangled. The production team heard you on Northern Focus and the demo tape, and based their decision purely on the quality of your playing and Dan's singing.'

Sarah put her arm spontaneously around Dan's shoulders and hugged him. The others remained in shock for several seconds before Martin Hirst spoke.

'You might not have arranged this, Frank, but we still owe it to you. We won't let you down.' There were loud calls of, 'Here, here.'

'I know you won't. There's one more thing I should mention, and this comes from Hutch as well as from me. It may sound strange after what I said earlier, but we don't want you to do this because of past unpleasantness. We want you to do it because you're professionals and because you were chosen for the job. You no longer have anything to prove.'

There was silence for a few seconds, and then Norman said, 'Frank's right. We were making a living as musicians before the others were born. We don't need to rub it in.'

'We certainly don't.' Geoff, of all people, was the first to agree.

'Right,' said Frank, 'let's go to the bar and celebrate.'

'Yes!' Kate punched the air and the others took up the cue in their several ways.

Sarah found Frank in the Club lounge. 'It's fantastic news,' she said. 'It couldn't have been better, and it *is* down to you, whatever you say.'

He shook his head. 'Dan clinched it for himself. They heard him and they wanted him.'

'But it was your contact.'

'OK, I'll accept that. Look, he's here now.'

'Thanks, Frank. I can't believe it.' Dan was still breathless.

'It's the perfect opportunity for you,' he agreed. 'They want someone who can sing new lyrics but still sound like a singer of the period. Mark Turner and Lionel Browning are writing the lyrics, and for my money they're the best in the business.'

'It's too incredible for words.'

'It must seem so,' agreed Frank, 'but you'll come down to earth soon enough when the hard work begins.'

'Right.' Still grinning with euphoria, he let Kate draw him away.

'Let's find a seat, Sarah,' Frank suggested. 'I'm not used to playing Santa Claus and it's wearing me out.' They found a corner table away from the others.

'They're good for each other,' said Sarah. She was looking at Dan and Kate, who had also found an unoccupied table.

'Do you think so?'

'Absolutely.'

'At least I know what's happening now. I could never keep track of her and her boyfriends before.'

'She was bored with young, immature boys, she told me, although I'm not sure I'd describe Dan as mature exactly, being as shy as he is.'

'He can be as shy as he likes for me.'

'Yes, it must be hard to let go. I hadn't thought much about it, but I suppose with everything that's happened it's only natural in your case.' She added hurriedly, 'Not that I'm prying, you understand.'

'You don't need to pry. You're a Hutchins, and it's impossible to keep anything from them. I learned that a long time ago.'

'Nosey parkers, the lot of us,' she agreed.

'But in a good way.'

She smiled. 'You'd better believe it, Blue Eyes.'

'You do a good Bogie.'

'I should hope so. He's been my lifelong companion.'

'But my eyes aren't blue.'

'So you've been miscast. Be thankful you were cast at all.'

'Sam Goldwyn?'

'Or Jack Warner or Louis B. Mayer. I forget.'

He looked over her shoulder. 'I'd give you my Gary Cooper but I think we're about to have company.'

'Thank goodness for that.' She looked round to see who was coming and saw Norman. He was looking less than his usual confident self.

'Frank, he said when he reached the table, 'You're a star and you've done wonders for us, but I've still got a little favour to ask you.' He hesitated. 'Actually, it's quite a big one.'

'What is it?'

'I wouldn't want to burden you ordinarily but I haven't much choice.'

'Go on then. Ask away.'

'I've got to go into hospital on Monday, just for a few days.'

'Really?' Norman was the last person he would have associated with illness. 'Nothing horrible, I hope.'

'No.' Norman shook his head to dispel the idea. 'They just want to do some tests. It's a load of nonsense in my opinion. I've been as fit as a butcher's dog all my life, and now they want to find something wrong with me. They want to do some tests on my circulation.'

'It's better to know about these things.'

'I suppose so, but the real problem is Ida. I wondered if you'd have her just for the three days or so. She's very fond of you and I know she'd settle with you.'

For a moment, Frank thought he'd misheard him. 'You want me to have her? Norman, I've never had a dog. I wouldn't know how to look after one.'

'There's nothing to it, Frank. All you need to do is feed her, water her and walk her. That's all. I'd ask Geoff or Hutch but they've both got cats, and Vernon's not so good on his feet, as you know.'

He shook his head. 'I'm not sure I'm the right one, Norman, much as I'd like to help you.'

'Aye well, I suppose it was a lot to ask, and I've no doubt you're busy enough already. Don't worry about it.'

Frank saw the disappointment in the old man's face, and Ida gazed innocently up at him. It was too much to bear. 'Oh, bugger it,' he said, 'all right, I'll look after her.'

Norman brightened immediately. 'Thanks, Frank. I hate to be a nuisance.'

'Oh, you're not, and it's probably a good time for me to have her. I don't have to go anywhere next week.'

'As I said, Frank, you're a star.'

'He feels miscast,' said Sarah, 'but I think you'll agree, he's not twinkling too badly tonight.'

## 24

On Monday the world seemed to be populated by disgruntled people. Helen told Frank that dog owners were social criminals who allowed their pets to spread disease, and that Robert agreed with her. Frank told her that someone whose job it was to rob honest people of their hard-earned money and who couldn't start a lawnmower was in no position to make judgements about anything. Helen hung up on him.

At visiting time, Norman told him that the other occupants of the ward were senile and that he was missing Ida.

Ida was missing him too. In between walks to keep her mind off things she lay in the studio nestled against one of Norman's old mufflers and looked forlorn. She ignored the canned beer that Frank put down for her so he was obliged to take her to the Coach and Horses for a half of draught bitter. He thought that might settle her but he was wrong. The whining began two minutes after he'd gone to bed and it continued until he was convinced that everyone in the block must be able to hear it. He gave her a dog treat – she had acquired the taste for them since her first fan mail – and he switched on the TV set, another of Norman's recommendations, but neither expedient made any difference. Each time he tried to leave her she whimpered again with unremitting grief.

At one-thirty his ingenuity was exhausted. He was stroking her and wondering if he should defy Norman's edict and take her to his room, when a last, desperate idea came to him.

He awoke several hours later with a stiff neck and a damp patch on his dressing gown where the spit had dribbled from his trumpet, but morning had arrived, and things always looked better in daylight. At least, that was what he told Ida.

Showered, shaved and almost human, he clipped her lead on and walked her to Reg's Take-Away for breakfast, which they took to the park. Ida had two rashers of bacon, and Frank had a large fried-egg-and-sausage sandwich. He felt that they were both due for a treat.

He took her to the bench by the war memorial. The private was still clutching his privates and his face was still set at the trees. The roses were still in full bloom as well. Months had passed since his chance meeting there with Norman, but little had changed. The old evergreens stood as proud as ever.

He finished his sandwich and lobbed the crumpled paper bag into a bin. A woman had stopped beside the bench. She was middle-aged and dressed for sensible shopping.

'It's going to be hot for the rest of the week,' she said, as if in answer to a question.

'I'm sorry?'

'You're miles away, aren't you? I said, the forecast says it's going to stay hot all this week.'

'Oh, that's good.'

'What sort is it?' The woman pointed to Ida. 'Heinz Fifty-Seven Varieties?'

Frank summoned his patience. If the woman really wanted to be insulting, he wondered why she didn't simply use the m-word. 'Actually,' he told her stiffly, 'she's an Albion Terrier.'

The woman looked doubtful. 'I can't say as I've ever heard of that breed.'

'There aren't many about.'

'Oh.' She advanced a step and looked at Ida with increased respect. 'She must have been expensive.'

'Very expensive.' He remembered Norman telling him about the vet's bill.

Ida moved forward cautiously and sniffed at the woman's shoes.

'Ida, heel,' he called. She returned immediately to sit to attention at his left foot. 'She belongs to an ex-guardsman,' he explained.

'Oh.' She peered at Ida again with new respect. 'Well I never. Well, I'd best be off if I'm going to catch that bus. 'Goodbye.'

'Goodbye.'

He fondled Ida's ears and was about to get up when he heard the sound of running footsteps. The sound came nearer and eventually the runner appeared from behind the memorial. It was the Candidate for the Promotion of Regional Produce. Clad as usual in a T-shirt and brief shorts, she was a sight to gladden the heart of a man sorely tried and low on sleep. She called out a friendly morning greeting and waved to Ida before skirting the central lawn and vanishing into the trees.

He stood up to go. Ida was worrying again so he told her she mustn't. She would see Norman sooner than expected if things ran according to plan.

On the way home he wondered idly if the Regional Produce Candidate often ran through the park at around twenty-past nine.

...

At two-thirty Norman looked anxiously at his watch.

'Visiting time's only just started,' Vernon reminded him. 'Don't fret, he'll be here.'

'Is there anybody about?' Norman gestured towards the nurses' station.

Geoff shook his head. 'They're all in the office having a brew.' He peered down the ward to make sure, and a few seconds later turned to Norman with a grin. 'He's here now.'

Frank looked carefully about him and crept into Norman's alcove, carrying a canvas grip and a four-pack of Tetley's bitter. Norman looked at him in expectant silence as he put the grip on the bed and unzipped it carefully. A small, white, tousled head emerged, followed by a joyously wagging tail.

...

Less than twenty hours later Frank embarked on his last morning's exercise with Ida. He led her to the end of Station Road, where she pulled him towards Reg's Take-Away. He bought breakfast for them both and they took it to the park, where she led him to the bench they'd used the day before and watched him expectantly as he sat down.

He took her bacon from its bag and fed it to her. It was a pleasant sort of day. The sky was slightly overcast, but it was warm, and there was no immediate threat of rain. As a dog minder he had to consider such things. He ate most of his sandwich before deciding that the burger was less appetising than the sausages he'd had the day before. He fed the rest to Ida and disposed of the bag, suddenly conscious that he was no longer alone.

'Hello.'

He turned to meet the newcomer. The shirt and shorts were different, but the effect was just as glorious. 'Hello,' he said.

'I'm not in the mood for running this morning,' she said. 'You can overdo it.'

Frank agreed with her. He couldn't actually remember the last time he had run anywhere but he was still familiar with the concept.

She squatted down to stroke Ida, who retreated behind Frank's legs. 'She's nervous,' she said, 'but it's not surprising really. It must be off-putting, being handled by a stranger like me.'

Frank took in her friendly smile and athletic figure and tried not to disagree with her. 'She's very nervous,' he said. 'She's a one-man dog and her owner's in hospital. I'm just looking after her until I pick him up later this morning.'

'Ah, in that case it really isn't surprising.' She rose to her feet and flexed her splendid, tanned limbs in turn before sitting beside him.

'She'll be all right,' he said. He saw that her hair was shingled and quite short, and she had a tiny brown mole beneath her left ear. It was early to be making plans, bearing in mind

Kate's feelings, but there was no harm in getting to know her. He already knew certain things about her. He knew from her election address, for example, that she was a lone parent and that by this time her son must be about eighteen.

'What's her name?'

'Ida.'

'She's lovely. Ida's a nice name too.' She wrinkled her nose in thought. 'There's a song about someone called Ida.'

'She's actually named after Princess Ida, in the operetta by Gilbert and Sullivan. The only other one I know is "Ida, Sweet as Apple Cider".'

'No, I don't know that one.' She lifted her left leg and crossed it over her right, and he noticed inconsequentially that the bench seat had left marks across her thigh. 'I was thinking of, "Ida Was My True Love When I Was Seventeen". She sang a couple of lines for him, and he was relieved when she decided to leave it at that. Whatever other charms she had beyond the obvious ones, she certainly couldn't sing. To be fair, neither could he, but it was still disappointing.

'No,' he said, 'I'm afraid I don't know that one.'

'Never mind.' She stretched out with her arms behind her head and eased her legs forward over the seat.

'Are you training for anything in particular?'

'Yes, I'm hoping to run the London Marathon.'

'I'm impressed.'

'It's not always easy fitting the training in, but I'm self-employed so I've got some control over the way I organise my time.'

'Great. What do you do?'

'I'm in outside catering. Parties and that sort of thing.' She said it quite dismissively, as if her work was of secondary importance, so he returned to the subject of running.

'Do you have a charity in mind?'

'Cancer Research.'

'Good for you. I approve of that.' He fumbled in his pocket and produced a card. 'Phone me when you're ready,' he said, 'and I'll sponsor you.'

'Oh, thank you.' She took the card and read it. 'What sort of music do you write?'

'Commercials, TV themes and film scores.'

'Right. I must have heard your music at some time. What have you done?'

He searched his memory for the most recent examples. '*Looking Back, Wings Over the Weald, The Private Life of Daniel Defoe…*'

She looked vague. 'Are they on ITV?'

'And Channel Four.'

'I watch mainly BBC, I'm afraid.'

'Don't worry about it.'

'I'm a musician too,' she said, possibly to soften his disappointment. 'I play the guitar.'

'Really?' He thought about her singing and an awful feeling crept over him.

'Yes, I play at The Black Bull most weeks. They have a folk night every Friday. You should come some time.'

His suspicion was confirmed.

'It's marvellous fun, and it's great socially. As a matter of fact it was the folk nights that got my husband and me back together.'

Frank bowed to cruel destiny.

## 25

'I'm grateful to you, Frank. I shan't forget this.'
'You're welcome, Norman.'

'Bringing her in was a brilliant idea. You don't know what that did for me.'

Frank silently agreed that the Trojan Grip had been one of his better ideas.

'I'm glad she was no trouble.'

'None at all. I'll see you on Sunday.' He put the phone down and uncrossed his fingers. There was no need to tell Norman that he never wanted to hear 'You Are My Sunshine' again, let alone play the damned thing on his trumpet. It was the third time the old boy had thanked him for having Ida. It meant so much to him.

He looked again at the fax on his desk. The lyric writers had pointed something out that had also occurred to him. He'd already phoned Patsy, who'd told him that the budget was there and that it was up to him to find a solution. He'd been about to arrange one when Norman phoned.

He dialled the number of Beckworth College and asked to be put through to Sarah. It seemed that long holidays were now a thing of the past. She answered straight away.

'Sarah Hutchins.'

'Hi, it's Frank. Is it a bad time?'

'No, it's a good time. I'm bored with what I'm doing. How's Ida?'

'Blissful. I brought Norman home yesterday.'

'Oh, good. Did they find anything?'

'Only old age. He's just got to take life more slowly.'

'That's not easy for him, or for any of them for that matter.'

'That's true. Listen, Sarah, I had a chat with the lyric writers about the new series this morning, and there's a tiny problem.'

'Oh, no.'

'It's nothing terrible. The thing is, you see, all three of us feel that there should be a female vocalist as well as Dan.'

'OK, I can see that, but to be honest, I can't really think of anyone who might be up to it.'

'I want you to do it.'

There was a pause of several seconds and when she spoke she sounded incredulous. 'But they haven't heard me.'

'I have, and it's my decision. I've just been told that.'

'Frank, I don't know. I could learn the existing songs from recordings. That's easy enough, but you mentioned some new numbers, and I'm not brilliant at reading music.'

'A lot of singers can't read dots at all. If it comes to that, they can't count beats either, but you're a dancer and you can. That alone gives you an advantage.'

'And you really think I could do it?'

'Of course you can. I'll take you through the new songs, or Vanessa will. No problem.'

'Are you really sure?'

'You take some convincing. Listen, sister, there are four Winchesters aimed at you. Throw down your shootin' iron and come out with your hands up.'

'Oh, Frank, that was the lousiest accent I ever heard but I'll forgive you for anything right now. Do you know what the existing songs are yet?'

'I've got a list. D'you want to come over and go through them?'

'When?'

'When can you come?'

There was a pause. Presumably she was checking her diary. 'I've got tomorrow free.'

'So come over, about ten or eleven.'

'Which?'

'Surprise me. It's Flat 2, Eden House, Providence Road, off Britannia Road, above the railway station.'

'… Britannia Road. I've got that. Gotta go, I'm afraid. The Vice-Principal wants me to play badminton with him and it's worth creeping points.'

'Fine. 'Bye.'

He put the phone down, wondering what Sarah looked like in badminton gear, and then wrote a fax to Mark and Lionel and another one to Patsy. She mustn't be allowed to think that he was indecisive as well as unassertive.

## 26

Sarah wore fitted jeans that fell away from the knee, and her legs were long and shapely, but as far as he knew she didn't strum an out-of-tune guitar and sing in a nasal, mock-Somerset accent, omissions that were strongly in her favour. He put the coffee things on a small table.

'Frank,' she asked, 'why did you have your hair cut short? I've been wondering.'

'It's a silly story.' He poured the coffee and beckoned to her to take a seat.

'They're the only kind worth hearing,' she said, sitting on the sofa. Come on, tell all.'

'OK.' He told her about his visit to the optician and the nightmare vision in the mirror.

'I'm not surprised.' She seemed to find his reaction quite natural. 'You'd have looked pretty silly like that.'

'That's what I thought.'

'But you don't. You look like a respectable bandleader.'

'Thank you.'

'You're welcome. She got up and went over to the bookshelves. 'Being a Hutchins and a nosy-parker,' she said, 'I always have to look at people's books.'

'Feel free.'

'I expected lots of technical books about music.'

'They're in the studio.'

'Of course.' She fingered the books on the top shelf. '*A History of the West,*' she read. '*Custer, Wyatt Earp, The Lawmen, The Gunfighters, The Outlaws, The North American Tribes, The Plains Indians, The Boys' Book of the Wild West*. May I?' She pointed to the last one.

'Be my guest.'

'This is a well-thumbed and well-loved volume.' She held it open and read the inscription. '"To Neville, with love from Mum and Dad, Xmas 1935." Do you collect old books?'

'Not now, but I did when I was a kid. When you're hard up they're as good as new ones. Neville was our next-door neighbour, except he was Mr Shaw then.'

She closed the book. 'I'm sorry, Frank.'

'It's all right.'

'No, that was really clumsy of me.'

'Don't worry about it.'

'She placed the book carefully on its shelf. 'Maybe we should make a start.'

'OK, bring your coffee through.' He got up and showed her into the studio. 'You take the chair. I'll sit at the piano.'

She sat down and looked around the room. 'So this is where it all happens.'

'Most of it,' he agreed.

'It's a closed book to me.' She thought for a moment and asked, 'Where do you find your inspiration?'

'I get that when I open my bills and bank statement. You can't beat them for concentrating the mind.'

'I shouldn't have asked, should I? It was probably a silly question.'

'You weren't to know, and it's a popular idea that composers sit around and wait for the muses to come up with the goods. Unfortunately, composing is mainly hard work, like any other job.'

'Oh dear,' she sighed. 'That's shattered an illusion.' She looked around the studio again and said, 'It makes sense though. There must be a lot more to it than just writing the music.'

'There is. First of all, I'm called to view a final cut of the film, play or whatever it happens to be. Then we do the "spotting". That's when we identify where the music's going to go and what kind of music it's going to be. After that, the music editor sends me the timing sheets that list all the cues and times, and when I get that I do the "laying out", which is when I set out the required numbers of bars and decide on time signatures and suchlike, and when I've done all that I can start thinking up the music.'

Sarah's eyes were glazed. 'Thanks for telling me that,' she said. 'Mind you, I'm still mystified, so you haven't ruined everything.'

'Good. There has to be some magic in our lives.'

'Life would be too awful without it.' She looked at her watch. 'But work beckons. Perhaps we should make a start.'

'Right,' he said, 'do you know this one? "It's Only a Paper Moon". It's a dead cert for one of the scenes.'

'I've heard it,' she said. 'It shouldn't be too hard.'

'OK, see how you get on. They'll only use the chorus so we'll concentrate on that.'

They worked on the song and then went on to look at two others, including Sarah's old warhorse: 'Embraceable You'.

Eventually, he said, 'Do you want to break for lunch? There's a pub just up the road that serves good food, if that appeals.'

'I find that very appealing, but I'm paying. You got lunch at The Copper Kettle.'

'That was on the house.'

'But the intention was there. You're not the kind of man who doesn't like a woman to pay her way, are you?'

'No, I'm the kind who usually does as he's told.'

'Good, that's settled.' She stood up and noticed a sheet of paper by her feet. She picked it up. 'It looks like your shopping list,' she said, putting it on the desk. 'Better not lose that.'

'I make lists all the time. My old trumpet professor gave me the idea. It's a way of coping with muddle-headedness.' He took the list and dropped it into the bin. 'Some people I know can arrange their thoughts in an ordered sequence, like a train timetable and with everything in perspective—'

'And some people have to work at it,' she agreed, 'but if their disorganised ideas come together to make wonderful music, what use is a timetable to them? Come on, let's go and eat.'

As they walked up the road she asked, 'How's the divorce progressing, if you don't mind my asking?'

'We should have the *Decree Absolute* by Christmas,' he said. 'That's if Helen's people stop nit-picking and accept the fact that I'm trying as hard as I can to be fair.'

'You strike me as a fair man, Frank. Possibly too fair at times.'

'Why do you say that?'

She laughed. 'Think of the grief you took from me. You were positively saintly.'

'Oh well, I'm hardly a saint.'

'Maybe not, but if all men were like you, women would rule the world, mark my words.'

'I thought they already did in a sneaky sort of way. Anyway, here we are.' They'd reached the pub and he took her in. 'What would you like to drink?'

'No way,' she told him firmly. 'If you go to the bar you'll give them your credit card or something. I'm paying.'

'OK, I'd like a glass of dry white, please.'

'Right. Do you want to grab a table?'

He went through to the restaurant and found a corner table. Sarah joined him presently with two glasses of wine. They looked at the menu and Frank settled for the sole. Sarah went to the bar again and returned presently. 'Done,' she said, taking her seat.

'Why am I so remarkable,' he asked, 'because I play fair?'

She considered the question and said finally, 'I know I shouldn't broad-brush the whole male population but it's difficult not to.'

'Is it because of what your father did to you?'

She nodded. 'That probably started it, although subsequent experiences haven't helped.' She arranged a beer mat square with the table edge and placed her glass on it. 'It's not surprising you thought I was a frump when I first came to band rehearsals.'

'Not exactly.'

'I bet you did, and I was. It wasn't a good time. To be honest, I wasn't prepared to get myself up like a fashion plate just because I was going to be among men. Frankly, I couldn't have cared less at the time what any man thought about me.'

'Oh well, that's your business.'

'No.' She held up her hand. 'You tell me things.'

'Surprisingly, but you're a Hutchins after all.'

'Right, and now it's your turn to listen.'

'All right.'

'I'd just come through the end of a relationship. It was rocky for some time but I thought we could work it out. I never expected it to end the way it did.'

'You don't have to tell me this.'

'But I will,' she insisted, 'so listen. I needed a blank videocassette and I found one without a label on the coffee table, so I put it into the machine to see if there was anything on it.'

'I think I can guess.'

'Probably. He'd filmed himself cavorting with his new girlfriend and he'd left the cassette where he knew bloody well I'd find it. It was easier than telling me to my face that it was over.' She shifted her glass and beer mat to the centre of the table. 'You wonder why you're different. Could you have done that?'

He shook his head. 'I get camera shy in a photo booth.'

'Oh, Frank.' Her expression told him that words failed her.

'I'm sorry, I've done it again.' He touched her hand. 'Sorry, sorry, sorry, I'm a prat. No, I wouldn't have dreamt of it.'

'You've got to stop doing that.'

'I'm really sorry.'

'I know you are. You're a nice man.'

'Thank you. I'm sorry you were treated badly. You don't deserve it.' He leant back to let the waitress set their dishes on the table.

'You *are* different from most men I've known,' She told him, 'and that's good, even though you make silly jokes when the conversation goes deep.' She thanked the waitress and reached for the tartare sauce. 'This halibut looks good.'

'I'm glad. It's odd though, going back to what you were saying about men. I know you've had some bad experiences, but you must have noticed a few exceptions. I mean you've got the greatest bloke in the world for a grandfather.'

'I know. He thinks a lot about you as well, and full marks, Frank. You said all that without making a joke about it.'

He smiled at the compliment. 'Once, when business was slow, I thought about being a stand-up comedian. I had the poor childhood and chronic in-law problem. It was just a pity I could never tell jokes.'

She sighed heavily. 'You use humour as a shield, don't you?'

'Sometimes,' he admitted, 'when feelings are out in the open. I suppose that's when I feel vulnerable.'

'Even when the feelings are someone else's?'

'Yes, when I can identify with them.'

'It's good to have a defence you can rely on,' she conceded.

'I think so.' He remembered Norman's observation about life in the depression years. 'Problems are there to be addressed,' he said, 'but there are times when there's sod-all we can do about them, and everyone has a defence mechanism of some kind.'

'OK, I'll buy that.'

'And sometimes a temporary escape route just happens, like a good idea or a shower of rain.'

'Or the right kind of music.'

He nodded. 'Bottled optimism. You can hear it in the titles.' He searched his memory. '"The Clouds Will Soon Roll By", "Beyond The Blue Horizon", "Hey, Young Fella"…'

'"On The Sunny Side Of The Street".'

'"The Best Things In Life Are Free".'

'"When The Red, Red Robin".'

'"Happy Days Are Here Again".'

'Don't forget "The Sun Has Got His Hat On".'

'It was on the tip of my tongue.'

It was evident that where the important things in life were concerned, they had little to argue about.

...

There was also agreement of a kind at Hutch's house later in the week, when his three companions gathered there. It was his turn to dispense hospitality, and as he handed the chocolate digestives around, two cats circled the group with their tails aloft, like hungry dodgem cars.

'Do cats eat chocolate biscuits?' Vernon was eyeing them with curiosity.

'If they get half a chance,' said Hutch, recalling a recent case of feline larceny. 'At least, they like to lick the chocolate off them.'

Norman wrapped a biscuit in a paper napkin provided for the purpose by Hutch. Because of the cats, Ida was temporarily confined to the car.

'Take her a fruit shortcake as well,' said Hutch. 'I know she's partial to them.'

'Thanks, Hutch.' Norman slipped one into the napkin.

Geoff had been silent for some minutes. Eventually he said, 'Who'd have thought last Easter, that we'd be recording music for a television programme by the end of the year?' He shook his head at the wonder of it all. 'It still seems too good to be true.'

'It does,' said Norman, 'but that's young Frank for you. He's a surprising lad.' There were sounds of agreement from the others, and then Norman said, 'You know, I'm not given to fanciful ideas as a rule, but I've been thinking about what they say, you know, about a bloke being born to perform one crucial job in his life.'

'Like Churchill,' said Hutch.

'Or Alf Ramsey,' suggested Geoff.

'Right, but what I'm saying is, I know young Frank's done a lot of good work over the last twenty years or so, but I can't help wondering if this might be his…' He searched for the right words.

'*Magnum opus*,' prompted Vernon.

Norman blinked.

'It's surprising,' said Vernon, 'what you can learn from the BBC in the middle of the night when you can't sleep.'

'So it seems. Anyway, I've just kept wondering if Frank's what-you-said is the band. You never know.'

'That's true,' agreed Hutch. 'You never know about these things, and I'm a great believer in destiny.'

'My mother always said I was destined for a life in music,' said Geoff.

The others looked at him with mild interest but little surprise. They'd known him for many years.

'I was born on a piano stool.'

Norman was impressed. 'That must have been a clever balancing act.'

'Well, almost on the stool,' Geoff conceded. 'It was when my mother was resident pianist at the Pavilion. That's the one that became the Picture Palace and then the New Vic—'

'Get on with it, Geoff,' said Hutch.

'All right. It was nineteen-nineteen, and she was nine months pregnant with me at the time. The film was *The Four Horsemen of the Apocalypse*.' He ignored the heavy sighs around him and continued. 'It was Rudolph Valentino's first big role, and when he came on the screen it was all too much for her. She went into labour and they had to take her into the manager's office. I understand the woman from the box office did the honours. She'd had a few of her own and she knew the drill.'

'She would,' said Norman, trying to remember how the subject had arisen in the first place.

'Anyway, they had to hold my mother down after the birth. Professional to the end, she was determined to see the film out.'

'They bred 'em tough in those days,' said Hutch.

Vernon narrowed his eyes. 'You didn't hang about. I'll say that for you.'

'What do you mean?'

'You must have been born on a bike, coming as quick as that.'

'I was never any trouble,' said Geoff. 'I was a model son.'

'Well, you had to get something right.'

'Be that as it may,' said Norman, returning to his original theme, 'Frank's doing a grand job for us, maybe the biggest job of his life, and at the same time he's got his living to earn. I just hope he's not taking too much on.'

## 27

Frank's workload was increasing. He had been asked for music for three commercials and received a commission from his old contact in Brussels for a theme for a new game show. It was also time to start work on the series. The scriptwriters were delivering their stuff and the existing numbers had to be re-scored for the band.

An unnecessary irritant, as he saw it, was that having completed his financial statement promptly, he found that Helen's solicitor was already asking questions about petty details. His solicitor had told him not to worry, but it was easy for him to talk. He was certain of one thing however, and that was that the money from Brussels was safe. It was a comforting thought, much needed because he was sure 'the other side' as his solicitor called them, had more grief in store for him. In that respect he was thankful that Kate was back in London.

The golden wedding gig was a pleasant distraction, even allowing for the extra Gershwin numbers he'd had to arrange, and the October Dance at the Exchange Club was even more welcome as a break from the increasing pressure he was experiencing.

Hutch came into the band room at the half-time break and tapped Frank on the shoulder. 'The "Embraceable You" number went well,' he said. 'Both Sarah and Dan are looking pleased, so the pressure's off there for a while. I think it's time to take a bit of pressure off you as well. I'll do the next few numbers while you take a break.'

'What for?'

'Because you need it. Just take a break and leave it to me.'

'What about "The Very Thought of You"? We need your tenor sax for that.'

'Dennis is going to do it. Now, be a good lad and do as you're told.'

Having no choice in the matter, Frank bought three drinks and joined Tim and Penny.

'That "Embraceable You" number was excellent,' said Penny. 'Wasn't that the girl who doesn't care for you?'

'She's OK, Penny. We're friends now.'

'No more penis envy?'

'It wasn't that, only a misunderstanding.'

'Oh good. Is Hutch going to go in front again?'

'Yes, he's laid me off for a spell.'

'Quite right, you look exhausted.'

'I'm OK.' He took a drink and watched the band enter the stand. It seemed an age since he'd watched them at the first dance, feeling their way, so apprehensive about their new venture.

Hutch announced a waltz.

'While I've got you here,' said Penny, 'we'll waltz for a change.' She let him lead her on to the floor to 'By The Sleepy Lagoon'.

'You're working too hard,' she told him.

'I'm thankful for it. Not all that long ago I was scratching around for work.'

'And now you've got too much.'

He shook his head. 'I'm not snowed under yet. I'll be all right as long as nothing else comes in before Christmas. The work's fine: it's this bloody divorce that's so wearing. The argument's only begun and I already feel like a cow that has to be milked twice a day.'

'So she's really going for what she can get?'

'It seems so.'

'But it's so unlike her.'

'It is, but she's no longer making her own decisions.'

'Of course.'

'Anyway, she can have her money as far as I'm concerned. I just wish the nit-picking and avarice were out of the way. Whatever happens to me now, I know I've done what I have to, and Kate'll be all right.'

She squeezed his shoulder with sisterly concern. They continued without speaking, their thoughts mutually understood and at the end of the dance he took her back to their table. He knew that the next dance was to be a quickstep, Tim's favourite.

He found Sarah at the bar.

'Hi,' she said, 'taking time out?'

He nodded. 'You were tremendous. Everyone loved it, and you looked great as well.' She still did because she hadn't yet changed out of the long, blue ball-gown that she'd worn for the number.

Frank looked round as Penny and Tim passed them. 'They've toned down their quickstep,' he said. 'They used to do all that skipping promenade stuff at one time. Very embarrassing it was too.'

'Who are they? I saw you dancing with her.'

'That's my sister and brother-in-law. I'll introduce you later.'

'I'll look forward to that. I must say they're pretty good.'

'There were Northern Ballroom Champions. My mother and I watched them on TV. It was black-and-white but we'd never known anything else.'

'And the presenters used to describe all the dresses, didn't they?'

'Oh, yes. "Couple Number Four"', he mimicked, '"are Tim Renshaw and Penny Morrison from Cullington in Yorkshire. Tim is an electrical engineer and Penny is an art student. Fortunately, her mother is neither of those things. She's a dressmaker, and just *look* at that dress. Penny told me that she and her mother sewed on all those sequins by hand."'

She laughed. 'Now I think of it, it must have been their photograph I saw in your studio.'

'Yes, it was that picture that gave me the idea of forming the band.'

'Really?'

'It was the only thing I could think of, and Wyatt and George seemed to be looking the same way. I took it as an omen.' He reckoned it was safe to mention that. 'You saw them in my studio.'

'I think so. Tell me again who they are.'

'Wyatt Earp and General George Custer. There was Billy the Kid too. He wasn't looking in the same direction but I know he was keen on dancing.'

She nodded understandingly. 'You'll have to come to my place some time and meet Bogie.' The quickstep ended and she turned to him. 'What's next? I know it's not me yet.'

'A rumba, then it's one of Dan's party pieces.'

'She looked up at the band and then at him. 'It's a real Indian summer, isn't it?'

'It's chucking it down outside.'

'I mean for the boys. I wonder sometimes how much longer they can keep it up at their age.'

'It's like the fountain of youth for them. They're more sprightly than I am tonight.'

'Is that why you're having a break?'

He nodded. 'Hutch's orders.'

They watched the dancers until the rumba ended.

He asked her, 'Can you foxtrot?'

'I think I could manage an approximation. I've watched it often enough and it doesn't look too difficult.'

'Not everyone would agree with you, but never mind. Would you like to give it a go?'

'You betcha ass.'

'Let's welcome Dan back,' said Hutch from the bandstand, 'to sing "The Very Thought of You". Take your partners for a slow foxtrot.'

The music began and they took to the floor. Not surprisingly, Sarah followed his lead, moving lightly and easily. The violet lights came up for Dan's solo and for the first time in hours Frank felt himself begin to relax to the gentle beat and the safe intimacy of the dance. He let his cheek rest against Sarah's and indulged himself in her scent and softness, luxuries he'd almost forgotten, and they danced like that until the end of the number, when he reluctantly broke away from her to applaud the band and soloist.

'So, how did I do?' she asked, affecting a hands-on-hips Mae West stance.

'Just fine, my little chickadee.' He would like to have said something witty, but his W.C. Fields was basic and his senses were jaded.

'In a few moments,' said Hutch, looking their way, 'Sarah's coming back to sing for us again.'

'Bloody hell,' she exclaimed. 'That's what happens when you get carried away.' She rushed over to the stand and Frank followed her.

'Don't worry about it, lad,' said Hutch, handing him the stick. 'You had a break and enjoyed yourself. That's the main thing.'

Frank took his place at the microphone and announced breathlessly, 'It's time for a quickstep. It's "Never Say Never Again, Again", and here's Sarah to sing it.' He started the number and looked across at Sarah, who rolled her eyes at him in mock relief.

By Monday morning, Frank was feeling more optimistic, at least about his workload. He still had two original songs to write, but the lyrics were good, and that was usually stimulus enough. If nothing more came in before the session, he felt he could cope.

He was working on the first of the songs when the phone rang. At least, he thought, it was too early for someone to be selling double-glazing.

'Frank Morrison.'

'Hello Frank, it's Lisa at the Midas Studio.'

They exchanged greetings and Frank knew exactly what was coming.

'We'd like you to do some arrangements,' she said.

## 28

The Exchange Club had not scheduled a dance for November, but practices went on as usual, mainly in preparation for the session.

Sarah sat back in her chair and nursed her drink. 'So what else have you been up to?'

'Work, lots of it. I shouldn't grumble, I know, but life is hectic just now.'

'And the divorce is a constant headache, I suppose.'

'More of a migraine, really. I'm been accused now of hiding information about offshore investments.'

She looked blank. 'I'm afraid I don't know what an offshore investment is.'

'I did a lot of work for Belgian television at one time,' he explained, 'and rather than bring the money into the country as a gift for the taxman I created a trust fund for Kate. Helen can't touch it, whatever she thinks. It's there for Kate to use over there or to do with it whatever she pleases.'

'I can't see anything criminal in that.'

'It's perfectly legal but that doesn't stop the other side asking silly questions about it, and the other piece of time-wasting is that Helen's seen an advertisement for a new release of seventies pop songs. It's got two of mine on it and she reckons I'm going to make a fortune in royalties. My solicitor's told the other side to grow up and be realistic, but the silliness goes on.'

'I didn't know you'd done any of that.'

'It was just before Kate was born and we needed the money. It's not my kind of thing at all. I didn't even write them under my own name.'

'Go on,' she said, 'tell all. What's your pseudonym? I'll buy the CD.'

'That,' he said, 'is classified information. It's too embarrassing for me to tell even a Hutchins.'

He was working well after midnight when the flat door opened. He swung round and saw Kate looking unusually deflated.

'Kate,' he said, 'I wasn't expecting you.'

'I know.'

'For heaven's sake, darling, what's happened?'

She put her violin case and grip down. With an unnaturally level voice she said, 'I'm here for the weekend. I want to get a practice in with the band before the session.'

'Good for you, but before that, have you got something for your elderly parent?' He knew from experience that an explanation would soon follow.

She reached up to kiss him.

'That's better. Would you like a drink?' He headed for the drinks cupboard. 'You look as if you could use one.'

'Please. I need a serious drink.'

'How serious, on a scale of straight-faced to deadly earnest?'

'Oh, Dad.' It was a sigh of despair.

'Sorry. How about a cognac? That's what I'm having.'

'Mm.' She nodded. 'Please.'

He poured two and asked, 'Soda?' It was an appalling way to treat cognac but she was his daughter and she was only nineteen.

'Mm.'

Deftly, he drowned the smaller measure with soda, at the same time noting with some alarm a resurgence of the word 'Mm'. It had been the all-purpose substitute for communication during her mid-teens and, delighted though he was to see her, he hoped he wasn't about to witness a relapse into adolescence. In his current state he doubted his ability to cope with it.

'I'm so pissed off it just isn't true,' she said abruptly, dropping into an armchair. 'There's no way I can stay in that house.'

'You don't have to.'

'I know. I only went back to keep you happy. I thought you had enough to worry about without, you know, trouble between Mum and me.'

'You should have told me. I didn't want you to make yourself unhappy.'

She took a sip from her glass, considered it for a second and then tried some more. 'It wasn't too bad when I went back in the summer,' she continued. 'Robert kept turning up but I could always go out and avoid him.'

'That's more than I can. I've just paid next month's instalment on my Poll Tax.'

'It's not funny, Dad.'

'I know, I'm sorry.'

'He was there tonight when I arrived.' She rolled her eyes upward and added, 'And he was there when I left. I mean, at *their* age.'

'Not the pleasantest thing to come home to, I can imagine.'

'You don't want to hear about it.'

'Don't worry about me. I came to terms with it a while ago.'

She looked at him for a while without speaking but he could see that she welcomed the knowledge. 'They're not living together,' she told him. 'They do sleepovers, just like kids at school. It's pathetic.'

'I'm sorry you had to come home to it.'

She shook her head. 'It's not just that. It's the way he's taken the house over. His belongings are all over the place, as if he owns it. He's left things in places that were, well, ours, and he's had the delinquents there as well, roaming all over the house.' Her eyes flashed angrily. 'They've even been in my room.'

'How do you know?'

''Cause they've drawn willies and things on my posters.'

'I didn't know that.' He wondered what else had been going on at the house. Helen must be out of her mind. 'You don't have to go back,' he told her again. 'It's up to you to please yourself where you live. You're right that I didn't want trouble between you and your mum, and I still don't, but you can't live like that.'

'Why do you have to be so *fair* about the whole thing?' She sounded like a scolding parent. 'No one's being fair to you. Let me tell you – and I think this is absolutely foul – her lawyer's going to screw you for everything he can get.

That's why it was so important for me to work last holiday, so that you didn't have to give me money.'

'Kate—'

'And if I can't get a grant I'll have to leave the Guildhall as well.'

'Hold on a sec.' He'd never appreciated how worried she was, and the realisation shocked him. 'The last thing you need concern yourself about is money. There's enough set aside to see you through the Guildhall and there's more besides. They can't touch that.'

For a moment she was stunned, and then she said, 'I'd no idea about any of this. I mean, you never said anything before.'

'I know,' he admitted. 'To be honest, it was one of those things that caused friction. It was a subject best left unmentioned.'

'What, the Guildhall?' She wrinkled her brow in disbelief.

'No, not that specifically. It was the whole business of investment.' He tried to put it tactfully. 'Some people find it difficult to trust others with their money, and for whatever reason, they criticise those who do.'

'I know. "Some folk are too clever for their own good, with their fancy London ways."' It was a creditable imitation of Helen's father, and her mother as well if it came to that. Kate had been more aware of the prejudice around her than he'd realised.

'But,' he said, 'I wasn't the one being clever. I paid an expert for advice.'

'And was it good advice?'

'It was excellent advice. Suffice it to say that it will eke out your pittance as a rank-and-file orchestral player very nicely. It should buy you a few luxuries as well.'

'That's fantastic.' She continued to stare at him, unable to believe her good fortune. Then she asked, 'But what about you? What will you do?'

'Don't worry about me.'

She thought for a moment and said, 'I could give you some of mine.'

'That's very generous of you but it won't be necessary, thank you. I'll be OK.' He hoped so anyway. It was nearly half-past one and his eyes ached with weariness, but at least he'd set her mind at rest for the present.

His mind wouldn't stop working, and he knew he shouldn't have had the third cognac. His eyes were dry with tiredness but his brain was alert. It was good that Kate and he had finally talked about something that had been going on for a long time, but now his memory was primed and making its own little journeys. By an odd sequence of connections he was back at the cottage in Birstall Lane with its stone-flagged backyard and outside lavatory. It was bitter out there in winter, even with the paraffin lamp beside the bowl to keep it from freezing. No one ever lingered on the throne in those days. Only the snow lingered, long after it was deep enough to play in. It seemed to hang on at the roadside long after the rest had thawed, gathering dirt until it was dark grey and no longer recognisable as snow. But it was exciting when it first fell. He would wake up and know immediately, even without looking, that there was snow, because everything was unnaturally quiet. There were none of the usual sounds, no traffic noise until the snowplough arrived.

By association he remembered the song he was working on when Kate arrived, the final one for the series. It was for a winter street scene, and the screenwriters were asking for a bizarre contrast between the scene and the song. Only that day, Patsy had mentioned its importance, and as he thought about Patsy an idea for a theme began to develop in his mind. After another minute he gave up on sleep, put his dressing gown on and slipped into the studio.

## 29
# December

Kate returned to London and would remain there until the eleventh, when she would join the band for the two sessions. Meanwhile, Frank worked, usually into the night. One morning he had woken up at his desk, having fallen asleep there some hours before.

Eventually he completed all his outstanding work and was then able to think about the band sessions.

Hutch had made the hotel reservations and organised a coach, or 'chara', as he called it, for the band, so Frank was relieved to find that there was nothing left for him to organise. The band would travel down on Monday the tenth, and return on the eleventh.

The only job that remained for Frank was the Exchange Club Dance on the Saturday before the session. By that time, he had forgotten how to sleep for more than two hours at a stretch and it seemed a good idea to get a taxi to the Exchange. He was sure he would sleep after the dance.

Unfortunately the taxi was late in picking him up, and he arrived at the Exchange Club with little time for social interaction. However, all the conversation at the half-time interval seemed to be about the downfall of Margaret Thatcher and the emergence of someone called John Major. In his exhausted state Frank cared even less than usual about party politics. The leadership struggle had passed him by and he had only the vaguest notion of who John Major was.

'You know,' said Geoff. 'He was Chancellor of the Exchequer. He's a quiet, serious kind of bloke, keen on cricket, and I can't help wondering if he might take a softer line than her before him. A more humane touch, you know. Less of that devil-take-the-hindmost attitude.'

Frank hoped so for his sake. For himself he was beyond caring.

'You look horrible,' Hutch told him when he caught up with him. 'Have you looked in a mirror lately?'

'I shave with my eyes closed nowadays.'

'I don't blame you, lad, it's a terrible sight. Give me the stick and go and have a rest.'

Without the strength to argue, Frank did again as he was told. Penny and Tim were elsewhere for the evening, so he went to the bar for a drink.

'Time out again? Don't blame you.' Sarah came and stood beside him.

'Would you like a drink?'

'Later, thanks.' She gave him a critical look, no doubt taking in the dark rings under his eyes. 'Why don't you go home? Hutch says he's happy to do tonight.'

He shook his head. 'I'll relax here for a while.'

'OK, you do that, my friend. I'm singing next, but I'll come down afterwards and find you if you like.'

'Fine, just so long as you don't miss your cue again.'

'Nope, it's my last number.' She walked away and disappeared into the dressing room. Frank found an empty table at the end of the ballroom and waited for her number.

Eventually Hutch announced 'Dream a Little Dream' and the music began. It was in the score for the series and it was important that it came over well. The boys were doing a good job and he felt guilty at leaving them to it again but he reckoned it was probably useful for him to listen occasionally from a distance. He wanted to hear Sarah as well.

Soon the blue lights came down over the floor and a white spot picked out Sarah at the microphone. She was wearing the pale blue dress that she'd worn at the last dance for 'Embraceable You'. 'Dream a Little Dream' was a different kind of song altogether, but Sarah was equal to it, and Frank listened, knowing he'd made the right decision.

She stood beside him after the number. 'You were asleep,' she said. 'I've brought you a drink.' She put a vodka and tonic down beside his half-empty glass.

'Thanks. I wasn't asleep, just resting my eyes. You sounded great.'

'Thank you. Have you heard from Kate?'

He nodded. 'She's a lot happier.'

'Are you coming on the coach on Monday?'

'No, I've got sessions either side of the band job. One in Chelmsford on Monday afternoon and the other in Slough on Wednesday, so I'll need my car.'

'You could get to those places by train, surely.'

'I know,' he shrugged. 'I just don't want the hassle of trains and taxis. I've got enough to think about.'

'OK. I'd offer to keep you company on the way down, but in view of the way things are with Kate I don't think it's such a good idea.'

'I'll be OK by then.'

'You'd better be.' She cupped an ear in Hutch's direction. 'The next one's a slow foxtrot. Are you game?'

'I'm game.'

'I'll hold you upright.' She took his hand.

'You've seen me swaying, haven't you?'

'There ain't much gets past me, and anyway, you look like a man who needs a bit of support right now. Let's just shuffle to this one.'

The blue lights came down again like partners in a conspiracy, and they moved together gently and closely, secure in the semi-darkness, to the muted, sensuous opening of 'Love Walked In'. He let his head rest against hers and realised in his sleep-starved state that this was what he'd been waiting for, the reason he hadn't gone home. He wanted to hold her close and enjoy the comfort and softness of her body next to his.

She began to sing along softly to the chorus. After a couple of lines she pressed her cheek to his, and at that moment it was the nearest thing to perfect bliss that he could imagine. On an impulse, he kissed the side of her neck and felt her draw him even closer.

They sat together at the end when the members and most of the band had gone. She put her hand on his and stroked it with her thumb. 'Have you got something to help you sleep?'

'No way. If I resort to that I'll never wake up.'

'Do be careful, Frank.'

He was about to say something meaningless again when he heard Hutch calling his name.

'Frank, are you there?' He hurried into the ballroom, clearly agitated. 'There's bother.' He took a deep breath and said, 'Bernard just nipped in to have a word after he'd packed his stuff away, and when he went out again his van had gone. It's been stolen with his drums and everything in it.'

## 30

The visitors' car park at Cullington High School was almost full by the time Frank arrived. Branch meetings were always well attended, with the new orchestra forming the majority, and he could only hope that the atmosphere would be pleasanter than of late. After the previous night's disaster the band members were in no shape to cope with any more strife. In particular, Bernard was distraught. His van and equipment were insured and could therefore be replaced, but to a professional musician all instruments were unique in some way.

Frank had spent the night going over the problem. To postpone the session was out of the question. The studio was booked for the day and the cost would still have to be met. Patsy would never allow that. The only possible course was to hire the equipment in London if they could, and even that would take time. The drums would have to be set up to produce the required timbre, and even though the boys were happy to work for as long as necessary, the studio would have to be paid for the extra time, supposing they could allow it. He wasn't looking forward to making that phone call to Patsy.

He took his place in the school hall and waited for Michael Tattersall to start the meeting. His heart sank even lower when he saw the faces of the other band members around him. It was as if the fight had been knocked out of them yet again. Elsewhere, members of the new orchestra acknowledged him with a solemn nod, and one smiled and shook his head sympathetically. The news had circulated swiftly.

He wondered just how much sympathy there was in the hall. There must still be a bond of some kind between musicians, and in his desperation it occurred to him that it had to be worth tapping, even if it meant eating a very large helping of humble pie.

Although the agenda was mercifully short, it seemed an age before Michael wrapped up Applications for Membership and asked for Any Other Business. Frank stood up immediately.

'Yes, Frank?'

'As you know, Michael,' he said, 'the band's travelling to London tomorrow to record the music for a TV drama.' Heads were bowed in embarrassment but he carried on. 'I think most of you know as well, that Bernard's van was stolen last night, along with the equipment that was in it.'

'Yes,' said Michael, 'we're very sorry to hear it.'

'Thank you. We appreciate that, but what I'm asking is does any of you know of someone who could possibly help us at this late hour?'

There was a growing murmur. Members turned to each other and conferred with those behind them. Graham Ellison, the new orchestra's percussionist spoke up.

'What are you short of, Bernard?'

Bernard, who had been staring at his feet throughout the meeting, looked up for the first time. 'Kit drums with hi-hat and crash cymbals, temple blocks, sticks and brushes,' he said, adding gloomily, 'it's a tall order.'

'It is,' agreed Graham. 'On the rare occasions when we need temple blocks we use the school's.'

'That's no problem,' said Rosemary Bentley. 'You can take them. I'll square it with the Head in the morning.'

Frank heard the intakes of breath around him. His plea had not been completely wasted.

'As for the rest,' said Graham, 'I'm not doing anything 'til the weekend, so if you promise to guard it with your life you're welcome to use my stuff. I'll bring it all round to the Exchange later on.'

# 31

Sarah saw the driver in the lobby. She imagined that he must have just returned from the coach park. 'Are you coming into the lounge?' she asked. 'Everyone else is there. I'm going to order tea.'

'That'd be nice.' He offered his hand. 'Name's Andy.'

'Sarah.'

'Pleased to meet you, Sarah. I heard you sing at Ferne House. I drove the band there. I took them to Bentley Hall as well.'

'Of course you did. I remember now.'

'The Ferne House gig was a great night.' He took the chair opposite her. 'When this job came in I grabbed it straight away. I wasn't going to miss the session.'

'Ah.' She was touched by his loyalty to the band but a shade apprehensive on his account. 'I'm not sure you'll be allowed into the studio while they're recording,' she said.

'Oh, I'll get in all right.' The way he said it gave her the impression that he might be difficult to refuse.

His eye fell on the personal stereo in her bag. 'What music have you got there?'

'*Smash Hits of the Seventies*.' Do you like seventies music?'

'It depends. What's on it?'

'A lot of good stuff. Do you like Cindy Freeman?'

'Yeah, she was great. What songs are they?'

'*Something Great is Happening* and *Stay With Me*.' She added almost to herself, 'Music and lyrics by William Bonney.'

He looked thoughtful. 'Great songs but I've never heard of him.'

Sarah had. According to the biographical dictionary in the college library William H. Bonney was much better known as Billy the Kid. She wondered where he was at that moment.

...

Frank was irritated. At another time he might have been angry, but he lacked the energy for that. Instead he was simply irritated. The Chelmsford session should have been easy and reasonably brief, but the late arrival of the vocalist and a series of unnecessary interruptions had meant that the recording was completed only within minutes of the contracted time. Consequently, he was obliged to negotiate the A12 during the worst part of the rush-hour and in heavy rain. It seemed to him that just for one day the world had become an altogether grown-up and unforgiving place. He felt justified in feeling irritated, and he stared moodily through the rain until his naturally philosophical disposition reasserted itself, prompting pleasanter thoughts.

One such thought that had seldom been all that far from his mind was the way in which Rosemary Bentley and Graham Ellison had come to the band's rescue. Graham, in particular, had surprised him. Instruments were more than just the tools of a musician's trade; they were his way of life, to be protected, guarded and treated with the greatest care, and to hand them over the way he had was an act of true generosity. It was a moment to be remembered.

After a lot of queuing and crawling through Central London he made it into Euston Road, where he spotted the hotel and drove into the car park behind it.

He walked into reception and dropped his bag and briefcase. 'Morrison,' he said. 'I'm booked in with the New Albion Dance Orchestra.'

The receptionist studied her screen. 'Mr Morrison,' she said, searching for the name. 'I can't see you here. Just a minute.' She scrolled through the screen and finally tapped his name in. 'No, I'm sorry. I can't find a reservation in your name.'

'But you must have.' Suddenly he was irritated again. 'Look,' he said, 'If you can't find the original reservation you must have a room somewhere that you can let me have.'

A young man came over from the other end of the desk and said, 'Are you Mr Morrison, sir?'

'Yes, I should have a reservation for tonight.'

'I'm terribly sorry, sir, it's my fault.' He consulted a sheet of paper and tapped something into the terminal. 'You're in room 314. There was a change of rooms. I deleted your name from one room and I'm afraid I was called away before I could re-enter it. I do apologise.'

'Well, now that it's sorted out I'd like to check in. I've had a foul journey and I'd like to have a shower before I eat.'

'Of course, sir. Actually a Mr Hutchins requested the change of rooms. He said you wouldn't mind. It seems he's superstitious about being on the third floor. Something about the war, he said.'

'That's odd. Anyway, I don't care which floor I'm on. I just want to check in.' He completed the form, took his key and went to look for Hutch in the bar.

The only person there was Sarah, and her relief at seeing him was undisguised.

'Hey Frank.' She kissed him. 'I'm glad to see you safe and sound. Hutch got your message and told everyone you'd be late. They've all gone in to eat. I thought I'd wait for you so that you wouldn't be alone.'

'That's really nice of you.' Incredibly he was beginning to relax already.

'Too right. My stomach's rumbling something awful.'

'I'd better book a table and then I'll freshen up.'

'I've reserved one. I freshened up as well. You're the only one with dust on his boots.'

'You look good.' She was wearing a mid-blue dress that he'd not seen before.

'Thank you. Now slope off and shave and I'll meet you down here.'

Half an hour later they were in the restaurant.

He asked, 'Have you seen Kate?'

'She's gone off with Dan in search of something livelier.'

'Good for her, even though the thought of it exhausts me.'

'Don't think about it.' She broke off a piece of terrine with her knife. 'You need all your strength for the onslaught tomorrow.'

'You make it sound like the Little Bighorn.'

'Oh don't say that. I saw what happened to Errol Flynn.' She added quickly, 'Not that I make a practice of watching violent epics. It was my boyfriend at the time who insisted on staying in and watching it.'

'Of course. He must have been OK, this chap. I mean there's not a lot wrong with a man who stays in to watch Errol Flynn. What happened to him?'

'Errol Flynn?'

'No, your boyfriend.'

'I can't remember. Maybe he went off with someone who had a posher video recorder than mine.'

'Bad luck. Has this happened before?'

'It's the story of my life.'

He patted her hand to console her. 'I've got a professional studio model.'

'Lucky girl.'

'I'm talking about my video recorder. I'll let you come over and use it sometimes if you like.'

'Frank, I'm just overwhelmed.'

'More wine?'

'We're three-quarters of the way down the bottle already.'

'I'll get another.'

'Does Orion pay for vintage Bordeaux?'

'Yes, Patsy just looks at the tabs and says what an expensive luxury I am and then she puts them through for payment.'

'You're just a charmer where women are concerned.'

'No, but it's nice to pretend.'

They chatted through the meal and eventually Sarah said, 'I never did ask you about Chelmsford. What went wrong?'

'It's a long, boring story.'

She considered that for a second and said, 'Save it for later. Tell me a short, easy-to-follow one instead, just for tonight.'

'I'd like to, but I'm too brain-dead.'

'I see everyone else has sloped off. Maybe we should do the same.'

They left the table and headed for the lift. He asked, 'Which floor are you on?'

'Third.'

'Me too.'

She fumbled in her bag and took out the key. 'Room three one three.'

'That's a coincidence.' He showed her his key tag for three one four.

'No, it's not.' They stepped into the empty lift and she pushed the button for the third floor. 'I overheard Hutch changing rooms with you because he was superstitious about the number. Something about the war, apparently.'

When they came to her room she stopped to run her finger under the raised digits on the door before turning the key. She asked, 'Are you superstitious?'

'Not really.'

'Neither is Hutch, the scheming old sod.' She took his hand and led him inside. 'Just wait 'til I see him.'

'I thought you weren't keen on men,' he said, drawing her towards him.

'Generally, no,' she confirmed, 'but I'm quite taken with this one.' She reached up to kiss him. 'Oh God,' she groaned, 'I thought this was never going to happen.' Gradually they progressed as far as the bed, where they sank down together. He struggled one-handed with the fastening of her dress, and with her lips still in urgent contact with his she managed to articulate the advice, 'It'sh a hook an eye an' a zshipper. You'd forgotten, hadn' choo?'

'It's been a long time,' he pleaded.

She disentangled herself and said, 'Hey, let's get the technical stuff out of the way, then it's free for all, OK?'

He nodded obediently, recognising an organised mind.

She unfastened the clasp and unzipped herself, then peeled off her stockings before pulling her dress over her head. He was already down to his shirt and shorts when she knelt on the bed to undo his shirt buttons. 'The bra fastens at the front,' she prompted helpfully, 'but come back to me if you have any problems.'

Mercifully, he was able to execute the task, so that when the tangle of arms occasioned by the temporary conflict of actions was resolved, her bra fell away to expose her small, neat breasts.

'Well done,' she said, 'you're getting the hang of it again.' She buried her fingers in his hair while he kissed her face, neck and shoulders and then journeyed downwards, marking his path with tiny kisses like stepping-stones. He crossed the flat plain of her stomach to the line of her briefs, where he changed direction to follow the lace border. She raised herself to slide the scrap of fabric down over her knees, finally flicking it away. 'I knew the lace would be a distraction,' she said. She performed the same operation with his shorts and then pulled him towards her. 'I don't know about... you,' she said, punctuating her words with hurried kisses, 'but I don't... really want to... wait... any longer.'

A moment later, she gave a welcoming gasp. 'Oh, Billy...'

Frank rubbed his eyes and raised himself on one elbow, fearful that he'd overslept. The display on the TV set told him that it was five fifty-four, which was a great relief.

Sarah lay naked under a single sheet, motionless apart from her regular breathing. He slid out of bed, taking care not to wake her, and went to the bathroom.

It was no surprise that the sight in the mirror was as awful as usual, although he must have slept longer than he had for weeks. He still felt jaded. The only difference was that he was happily jaded, and that was a big difference. He flushed the loo and washed his hands and face, and then spotted a bottle of mouthwash among Sarah's things. After a second's thought, he tipped some into an unused tooth glass and swished it around his mouth, remembering not to gargle. He would tell her later, after he'd made tea.

He topped up the kettle and had just flipped the switch up when she began to stir.

'Who's that strange man in my bedroom?'

'Frank Morrison, composer, arranger and bedroom-hopper.'

'That's all right then.'

'I've put the kettle on.'

'I knew you were perfect.' She raised herself on the pillows, lifted the sheets to cover her upper half and then let it fall again, leaving one breast delightfully exposed. 'As soon as I woke up,' she said, 'I said to myself, there goes perfection on three legs.'

'Two.'

'A trick of the light, perhaps.'

'It's quite normal really.'

'It played a big part in a very important scene.'

He walked over to the bed and kissed her on the lips before bestowing the same on the exposed breast.

'You're quite keen on them, aren't you?'

'Completely smitten.'

'I'll bring them back in a minute.' She lifted the sheet and slipped off the bed.

'Tea or coffee?'

'Tea, please. Milk, no sugar.'

While she was in the bathroom he busied himself with the miniature tea set. He was glad that she didn't take forever to wake up and have to be crept around for fear of creating a morning row.

'I nicked some of your mouthwash,' he confessed when she came out of the bathroom. In mitigation he added, 'I put the cap back on.'

'And you put the seat down, which bears out what I said about perfection.' She took the cup of tea he offered her and got back into bed. He slid in beside her.

'I'm sorry it was a bit short-lived last night,' he said.

'So it was a quickie. What's wrong with sprinting when you're in a hurry? Sprint one day and run a marathon the next, I say. Let some variety into your life, and anyway, who cares? It was great.'

He was thankful for that. Just one matter remained. 'Who's Billy?'

'Mm?'

'You mentioned him last night, just a few times.'

She gave him a sly, corner-of-the-eye look and sang softly, '"Something great is happening…"'

He realised that his last secret was out.

...

'Can we do a couple of numbers as a practice? The singers have never recorded before and I think the musicians would appreciate it too.' Frank was buoyed-up with adrenaline and in control again, at least for the time being.

'OK, Frank.' The engineer let the system run and Dan sang 'I'll String Along With You', followed by Sarah with 'Dream a Little Dream'. They both sounded pretty good to Frank. He looked around at everyone. 'Is everybody OK?'

'It's just like old times,' Vernon told him. The others smiled their agreement.

'Sarah and Dan, are you ready?'

They nodded.

'Right. Let's try "I'll String Along With You" again and see how it goes.' They played the number again with Dan giving his usual, sincere performance, and the first track was recorded. To give him a break they turned to Sarah and 'Paper Moon', which also went smoothly.

It was a straightforward session. Frank was pleased with 'Feeling Blue and Longing for Your Smile', the last song he'd written. He'd had problems with the middle eight until he was reminded of Patsy's unique phone greeting. It had given him his first four notes and the beginnings of a rhythm. The rest was straightforward.

It was a cheerful party that Frank saw on to the coach afterwards. They would return in the new year to record the remainder of the score and deal with any hitches that might have cropped up in the meantime, but it was that first day in the studio that most of them would remember.

Kate accepted a kiss shyly because they were in public, and then said, 'Remember to do as you're told, Dad, and take it easy. I'll see you on Thursday.' He watched her go and wondered for a moment. It seemed an odd thing to say but it went out of his mind when he shook hands with Vanessa and Thomas, who boarded the coach together, both looking particularly pleased with life. He shook hands with Hutch and Norman, and then everyone was on board. Somehow, in all the confusion, he'd missed Sarah. He was disappointed but he knew he would be seeing her soon and he had a lot to do in the meantime.

As the coach drew away he stood in the doorway of the studio trying to assemble his wits before deciding what to do next. The difficulty was that the adrenaline rush was now in full retreat, leaving him drained and helpless. His overworked brain had gone too long without rest and his longest sleep in weeks had amounted to no more than six hours. Perversely, he'd spent those hours of unconsciousness in the company of a delightful and fascinating woman. It was rotten timing.

A wave of extreme tiredness swept over him, leaving him with a tingling sensation in his arms and legs and the realisation that exhaustion had finally overtaken him. His car was at the hotel in Euston Road, literally just around the block, and he knew he was incapable of driving it. He wondered feebly about leaving it there until he was fit to drive again, but the idea refused to stay in his mind long enough for him to work on it. He leaned helplessly against the open door in abject despair.

'A cup of tea might be a good idea,' a voice suggested.

He turned in the doorway and stared, unable for the moment to believe what he saw. Finally he said, 'Sarah, what on earth are you doing here?'

'That's not much of a welcome.' She put her arms around his neck and kissed him as a mother might kiss a vulnerable child. 'The official line is that I have business in London. Actually, Hutch and a few of the boys decided that someone had to stay with you. I had a couple of days to spare so I volunteered.' She grimaced. 'Life's tough, but someone has to take these jobs on.'

He held on to her, struggling to make sense of what was happening, his relief at being no longer alone at odds with other concerns. Finally he released his hold on her and asked, 'Does Kate know?'

Sarah nodded. 'She said, "Take care of him." So relax, because that's what I'm going to do. I'm here to keep you company, and if at all possible, to keep you awake behind the wheel. That's unless you're happy to be driven by me, which is the really exciting option.'

He stared at her, still recovering from the surprise.

'Honestly,' she said, 'Kate and I aren't the only ones who are worried about you. Let's go back to the hotel and have a cup of tea before we do anything else.' She took his arm and led him in the direction of the hotel.

'I don't understand,' he confessed. 'You say Kate's in on this?'

'Yes, and she thinks it's a good idea.'

It sounded incredible. 'Do you think... she's twigged anything?'

'No, Frank.' She patted his arm like a reassuring parent. 'She knew we'd had dinner together, she saw us come down to breakfast together, and she knows we're going to be together for the next two nights, but I'm sure she doesn't suspect a thing.'

He stopped outside the hotel doors, oblivious to the rain that had begun to fall, and still unconvinced. 'It's just,' he argued, 'after her mother—'

'Frank, it's chucking it down. Can we go in.' She pushed her way through the revolving door and he followed. 'She's all right with it, trust me.' She led him to a table and two armchairs next to a newly-erected Christmas tree in the lounge. 'Kate's drawn her own conclusions about last night, and judging by her reaction when I told her I wanted to stay and keep you company, I'd say she's not at all perturbed. More relieved, I'd say.' She caught the attention of a waiter and ordered tea. 'After this,' she went on, 'I suggest we find the hotel in Slough and check in as quickly as possible so that you can hit the sack.' She looked at him meaningfully and added, 'I'm talking about sleep now, as much as you can get before tomorrow.'

Frank sank back into the chair, dimly conscious that a load had been removed from his mind. After a few moments, he said weakly, 'I can't believe this is happening.'

'Get used to it, Frank. This year's been all about you doing things for the boys, for Dan and for me, and now that you've worked yourself into a state of exhaustion for us, I reckon it's time one of us did something for you.'

...

He had only the vaguest recollection of the next few hours. All he knew was that Sarah had driven them to the hotel in Slough, and that having found their room he had lost consciousness within seconds of his head touching the pillow.

The resulting nine hours' sleep and an obliging vocalist made the Slough session mercifully easy although recovery was still far from complete.

Much later they lay together in the darkness of their room.

'Sarah.'

'Mm?'

'Could I have my arm back? You're lying on it and it's gone all tingly.'

'You know,' she said, raising herself to release the captive limb, 'you're just a hopeless romantic. I play the village maiden for you, I let you have your fiendish way with me, I make the kind of gratifying noises you haven't heard for months on end, and you demand the return of your arm. How flattered can a girl be?'

'Demanding wench.' He raised himself to look at her squarely. 'I flatter you with me body, damn it. Do you presume to demand flowery words of courtship as well?'

'Begging your pardon, milord, I'm sure, and I 'ope as 'ow your 'umble servant's unreasonable remark 'as not given rise to feelings contrary to them what got your lordship into this 'ere 'aystack with me in the first hinstance.' She cowered convincingly.

'Forgiven.' He patted her backside to confirm it. 'And you're half right about the romantic thing.'

'Only half right? That doesn't sound like me.'

'No one can be a romantic all the time. The real world doesn't allow it.'

'You have to be practical,' she agreed. 'Otherwise you could find yourself doing something downright unreal, like driving two hundred miles to London in a state of exhaustion.'

'That,' he said sadly, 'was down to temporary insanity brought about by the exhaustion.'

'So it's not likely to happen again?'

'Most unlikely, I'd say.'

'Good.' She traced a furrow with her finger across the hair on his chest. 'So when you're not being a romantic and you're not out of your mind with exhaustion, I take it you can be quite sensible?'

'That's right. I maintain a balance. I'll give you an example.'

'Please do.'

'It's something that happened when I was a student in London, twenty years ago.' He slipped his arm around her again and let her head rest on his shoulder so that he could tell the story properly. 'I can't remember just how it came about, but I was in the West End and I happened to be across the road from the Theatre Royal in Drury Lane when the stage door opened suddenly and out stepped Ginger Rogers.'

'You're kidding.'

'No, she was starring in a show there. I think it was *Mame*. Anyway, she'd be in her late fifties by then but she was still beautiful. At least, I thought so. I couldn't believe my eyes.'

'Did you speak to her?'

'I wanted to, quite desperately, but I was so shy in those days it was as if my feet were set in concrete. I just stood there, staring and pathetic, and then a taxi came and she got in. That was the last I saw of her.'

'Hell, Frank, that's tragic.'

'I know.' He stroked her hair idly, remembering his feelings at the time. 'I used to cringe when I thought of it, but eventually I had to admit to myself that I'd known the truth all along. It would have been great if I'd been able to speak to her and maybe tell her how much I'd enjoyed her films, but the fact was that it wasn't really Ginger Rogers that I'd been so desperate to meet. It was the characters she'd played. They were the ones I was in love with. You see, I can dream as well as anyone, but I can't go through life regretting an impossibility.'

'That sounds like a healthy balance to me.'

'Mm.' Tiredness was stalking him again but it seemed that his mind was set on exploring the subject. He had no alternative but to go with it.

'But I think,' he said, 'that we're all conditioned during childhood to believe in the impossible.'

'True,' she agreed. 'With examples like lucky old Cinderella and jammy little Snow White, what else were we to believe?'

'Exactly. We learn that if we're up against it for long enough, then by some kind of justice born of destiny, things will suddenly come good for us.'

She nodded. 'Riches go to the most deserving.'

'And we spend the rest of our lives learning the truth. We ask ourselves repeatedly if there's any justice in life, and we know damned well that if there is, it operates purely at random.'

'But we can spend half a year living in the happy-ever-after world of romantic song without getting cynical.

'It's true, and I still catch myself expecting good things, like bad ones, to come in threes. It's funny, isn't it?'

'I wonder. Most superstitions are based on experience.'

He eyed her with difficulty, partly because of the angle of his vision and partly because his eyes were closing again with tiredness.

'You never know, Frank,' she said, 'someone might easily come up with statistics to prove it, some time when there's a dearth of the usual kind of news.' Her voice softened when she realised that he was falling asleep. 'I wonder how things are going to work out for you,' she murmured, 'because by my reckoning you're well overdue for a bit of luck.'

His eyes had closed and he knew that sleep was about to overpower him. It seemed to him that one wonderful thing had already happened, and that was quite enough for the time being.

## 32

'We were really worried about you. You didn't have a clue about the state you were in, and neither did I at first, but Hutch said something and then Norman said the same thing and I knew something was wrong. What were you thinking of?' If Kate had learned anything from her mother it was how to turn a welcoming home into a bollocking. He shook his head, at a loss for an answer.

'I was going to stay with you,' she went on, 'but then we decided—'

'Who decided?'

'Hutch, Norman, Sarah and I, plus a few others. It was a sort of committee. We decided that you'd take more notice of Sarah.' She underlined her last remark with a knowing look.

'So you knew already?'

'It was pretty obvious, wasn't it?'

'I suppose it must have been.'

'You didn't exactly cover your tracks,' she said, 'not that you needed to.'

'So you don't mind?'

'Of course not. Sarah's my friend, although it beats me what she sees in you.' She smiled sweetly to let him know that she wasn't entirely serious. 'And there's a world of difference between Sarah and The Sheriff of Nottingham.' Suddenly she grinned. 'And speaking of which—'

'Whom.'

'Whatever.' Her glee was unabated. 'Robert,' she announced triumphantly, 'is no more! At least, he still exists, worse luck, but not as we knew him.'

'What are you saying?'

'I'm saying that they had the most manic row – something to do with the delinquents – but anyway, she dumped him. I went over there today and there was no sign. No Robert, no delinquents, not a trace. It's great!'

Frank was naturally in agreement but he had to show some sensitivity. 'How's your mum taking it?'

'I think she feels a bit flat but she's bound to see the situation for what it is. I mean, OK, she's lost a total plonker but she's regained her sanity.'

And her daughter, thought Frank, although he kept that observation to himself. He was sure that Helen would find someone else before long, but with one experience behind her Kate would be better prepared when the time came. Meanwhile, as he told Wyatt Earp later that evening, she was close to being reconciled with her mother. 'Another good thing,' he said. 'That makes two, and what more could a man reasonably want?'

...

'I think we should do something for young Frank,' said Norman.

'I've been thinking about that as well,' said Hutch. He transferred the phone to his left hand so that he could continue writing his shopping list. He was expecting Sarah shortly and he wanted to have it ready for her.

'It's just a question of what.'

'It was always a problem when he was a lad.'

'Aye, I know you and Ellie had a lot to do with both him and Penny when they were kids.'

'Quite a lot, yes.'

'Maybe we could put on a bit of a celebration. What do you think?

'We have to be careful, Norm. He's easily embarrassed if all the attention's on him.' Hutch was thinking; in fact he was thinking so hard that he was silent for longer than he realised.

'Are you still there, Hutch?'

'Yes, I'm still here.'

'I thought you'd nodded off.'

'No,' Hutch assured him, 'I've had an idea, and unless I'm greatly mistaken it's something that'll give a lot of pleasure to Frank and a few others besides. That's if we can bring it off.'

...

At Hutch's insistence, Frank missed band practice on Sunday morning. Instead, he found himself in Sarah's kitchen, picking up a tea towel after a late breakfast and watching her bum wiggle as she washed the dishes. His mind went back to the time he'd watched Helen mixing gravy. It was on the day of the first band practice and now he was in a different kitchen, watching a different bum, and it all felt right. Everything was right: the band was functioning without him, Kate was shopping with her mother – an encouraging sign – and Sarah's bum was wiggling. Suddenly life was good. He picked up a plate to dry it and the phone rang.

'It was too good to last,' said Sarah, drying her hands and going into the sitting room to answer it.

Frank carried on drying under the steady gaze of Humphrey Bogart. The picture was a still from *The African Queen* and, unbidden, the score came to him. He sang along as he dried the dishes. 'Chug-a-chug, chug-a-chug, chug-a-chug, chug-a-chug, chug-a-chug-chug-chug-chug-chug, dah, dah, dah...' The African Queen had negotiated a mile of river, watched by impudent monkeys and bored hippopotami, and was heading flat-out for white water when Sarah interrupted its passage.

'It's Hutch,' she told him from the doorway. 'He thought you might be here. He wants to speak to you.' She looked very pleased about something. It was either that or she was stifling her laughter at his singing. It had that effect on people. He took the phone from her and exchanged the usual greetings with Hutch, who sounded very pleased.

'I thought you'd like to know,' he said, 'they've found Bernard's van and drum kit, intact and in good order. The rest of his equipment had been jettisoned, unfortunately, but it was the kit that bothered him most. It was being kept in a lock-up in Batley. It's funny how it came about.'

'Great.' It was yet another piece of good news. 'How did it come about?'

'One of the thieves got talking to a chap in a pub in Batley and found out that he did a bit of drumming, so he told him about a kit he'd got for sale. He said he had a few other things as well, including a six-year-old Ford van in good condition. Ideal for gigs, he said, and that was what got this chap thinking. You see, the thieving sod didn't realise he was talking to an off-duty bobby.'

'Fantastic, but you said *one* of the thieves. How many were there?'

'Three, and this is the best bit. Guess who they were.' Hutch was obviously enjoying himself.

'I've no idea, Hutch. You'll have to tell me.'

'Remember the three yobs we caught terrorising little Julie in Albion Street?'

'Not them?'

'The same. They knew we were in the Exchange and they knew the van was connected with us so they stole it, more out of spite than greed.'

'Well I never. I hope they put the buggers behind bars.'

Hutch chuckled. 'I think it's more than likely. Anyway, I thought you'd like to know. Bernard's like a dog with two bones.'

'I expect he is. Thanks for telling me, Hutch.'

'No trouble, lad.' There was a pause, and then he asked almost as an afterthought, 'Have you got anything fixed for next Saturday evening?'

'I don't think so.' He knew that Sarah would have told him if she had anything planned.

'Good, because we're having a party at the Exchange, seeing as it's nearly Christmas and we've got things to celebrate anyway.'

'What kind of party?'

'Oh, a dance, some food and drink and that sort of thing. Spouses will be welcome, as always. Vanessa or Fred will cover on the piano if any of the band want to dance. There'll be Club members there as well, and we've invited Penny and Tim.'

'So it's informal.'

'It's black tie, but no one's standing on ceremony. Oh, and bring some female company. That granddaughter of mine will do nicely. She knows about the party.'

## 33

That Sarah had taken longer than usual to prepare herself for the party meant nothing to Frank. As he saw it, it was normal behaviour for a woman to spend an age in front of a mirror, and in any case he was delighted with the result. The pearl-grey satin ball-gown, an early Christmas present from him, was perfect, and the rest was no less perfect in his eyes. They would be late, he realised, and at another time he would have been anxious, but he knew that the party was to be an informal gathering and that Hutch would be in control.

In fact, it wasn't until he entered the band room and found everyone lined up and facing him that he knew he'd been set up.

'We know you don't like a lot of fuss,' said Hutch, detaching himself from the others. 'That's why we thought we'd do this before the party begins. All the usual crowd are here and there's a few more besides, but before we go in and join them we'd like you to accept this token of our gratitude for everything you've done for us.' There was a burst of enthusiastic applause as he handed Frank a silver baton in a presentation box.

Dumb with awkwardness and emotion, Frank read the inscription on the box. He had half-expected something of the kind to happen before long, but now he was unable to speak.

He looked helplessly at Hutch, but his salvation came from another quarter as Dan, followed by Kate and Julie began to sing 'For he's a jolly good fellow.'

The singing gathered volume with the rest of the band joining in. By the end, Frank had recovered some control over his voice.

'Thank you,' he said. 'Thank you all very much.' It was hopelessly inadequate, he knew, but the words refused to come to him.

'As I told you,' said Hutch, 'we've put on a bit of a party. It wasn't easy at short notice, what with the Club's usual caterers already booked for another job, but we found a firm that could do it, and the buffet looks pretty inviting to me. It's all good, local produce as well. It's a firm that specialises in it.' He hesitated and smiled. 'Oh, there's something else, Frank. There's another reason why this lot are looking as if Christmas has come already, and you'll see what it is in a few minutes when Sarah takes you into the ballroom, but just for now we have to leave you.'

They tuned to the piano, and when Hutch was satisfied, made their way up to the platform, where the applause, the footsteps and shuffling of chairs took Frank back to midsummer and the heady excitement of the NADO's first gig. Six months had passed since that event, and much had taken place in that time. He was just a little apprehensive about the nature of Hutch's surprise.

At the start of 'The Sun Has Got His Hat On' Sarah took his arm. 'It's all right,' she said. 'The embarrassing part's over. You're going to enjoy this.' She gave his arm a reassuring squeeze, and with absolutely no idea of what to expect, Frank followed her into the ballroom.

There was so much to see when he stepped through the doorway that he had to pause for a moment to appreciate it all fully. He was conscious first of all of the Christmas decorations, including a huge tree that stood by the entrance. It was as if Christmas had crept up on him while he was distracted, and had suddenly stepped into his path, huge and impatient to begin. He also noticed the buffet, laden with, according to Hutch, the kind of local fare that had won Frank's vote so convincingly at the general election. That pleased him too.

There were far more people than he had expected to find, and for a moment he was unable to identify individuals. Gradually, however, he began to pick them out. There were people he'd seen regularly at dances, members of the Exchange Club and their guests, and somewhere among them he saw Penny and Tim waving to him.

Such a gathering was surprise enough, but there were others too, people he'd never expected to see in the ballroom again, and who were all the more welcome because of it. He swallowed hard and took a deep breath as Michael Tattersall came over to him and shook his hand.

'Hello, Frank,' he said. 'I expect you're wondering what we're doing here.'

Actually, Frank had a pretty good idea and it filled him with pleasure in a way that few things could, but he let Michael continue all the same.

'The fact is,' said Michael, 'some of us had a meeting last Sunday morning with Hutch and a few others from the band, and we decided it was time to call a halt to the silliness. The orchestra and the band are happy, each doing our own thing. There's no need for ill-feeling.' He offered his hand again.

'Anyway,' he said, 'we've come along tonight to congratulate you and the band on all you've achieved, and to build a few bridges as well.'

Once again Frank found himself unable to express his feelings. He could only take Michael's hand and acknowledge such members of the new orchestra as he could see. Then, as a merciful distraction, Hutch appeared at the microphone to welcome everyone to the party.

From Frank's point of view it was the most perfect party, and it continued to be so to the end of the evening, when the last dance was announced. Fred's guitar led softly into 'Goodnight, Sweetheart' and Frank and Sarah took to the floor.

After a while he allowed himself a glance around the room. Kate and the boys were completely involved in their playing, and couples on the floor drew ever closer, as they always did under the spell of Ray Noble's music. Even the Candidate for the Promotion of Regional Produce swayed to the gentle beat as she gathered the empty dishes.

It was as Norman had said all those months before. You just couldn't beat it.

THE END